SUPERMAN® FAMILY ADVENTURES™

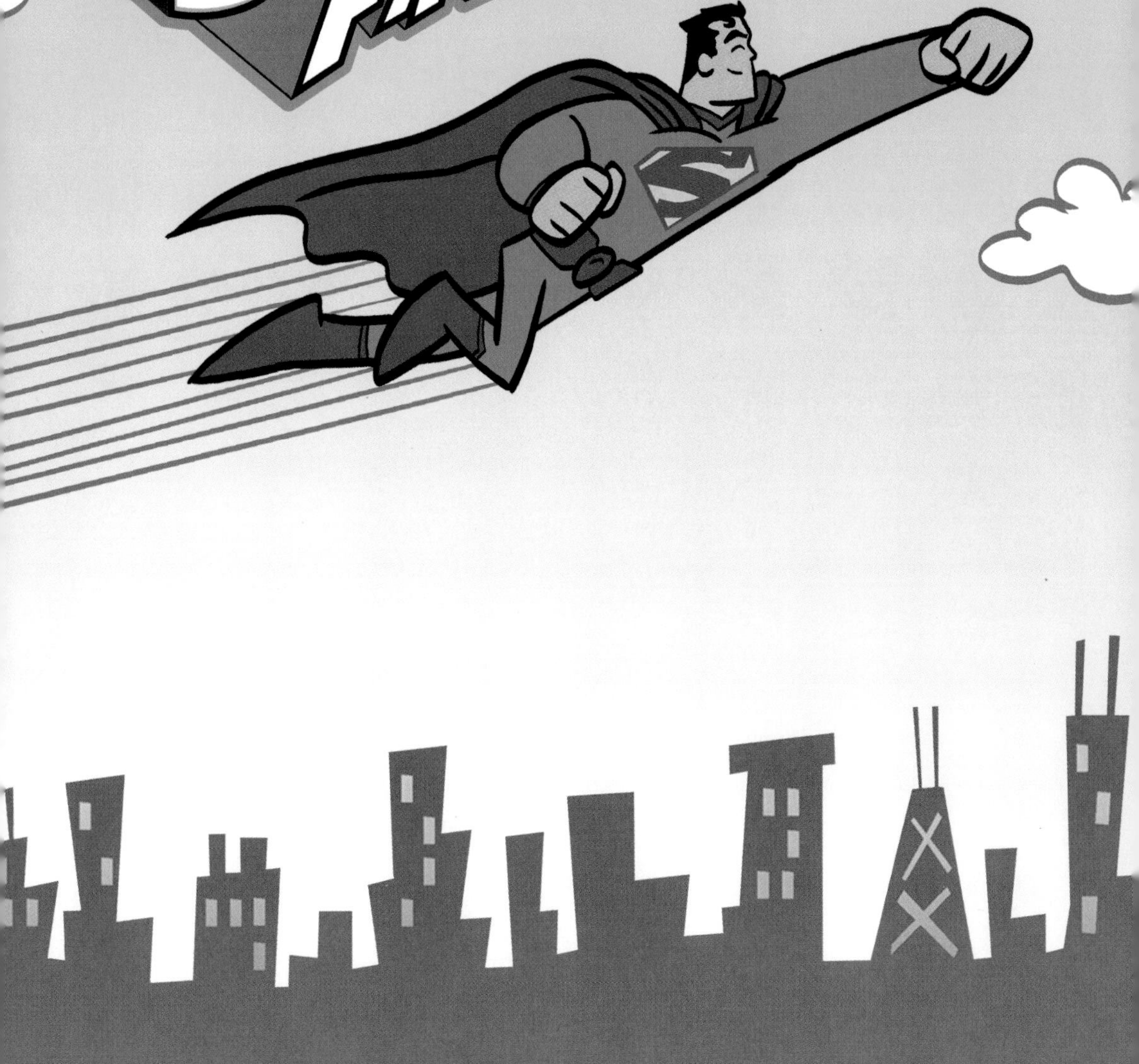

STONE ARCH BOOKS
a capstone imprint

STONE ARCH BOOKS™

Published in 2013
A Capstone Imprint
1710 Roe Crest Drive
North Mankato, MN 56003
www.capstonepub.com

Originally published by DC Comics in the U.S. in single
magazine form as SUPERMAN FAMILY ADVENTURES #3.
Copyright © 2013 DC Comics. All Rights Reserved.

DC Comics
1700 Broadway, New York, NY 10019
A Warner Bros. Entertainment Company

Cataloging-in-Publication Data is available at the
Library of Congress website:
ISBN: 978-1-4342-4792-6 (library binding)

Summary: What is Jimmy Olsen's Supergirl Theory? The sky is filled
with Super-Pets! What's up with Jimmy's wristwatch? How does that
thing work? Oh yeah, there's also an appearance by Superman!

STONE ARCH BOOKS
Ashley C. Andersen Zantop Publisher
Michael Dahl Editorial Director
Donald Lemke Editor
Brann Garvey Designer
Kathy McColley Production Specialist

DC COMICS
Kristy Quinn Original U.S. Editor

Printed in China by Nordica.
0413/CA21300442
032013 007226NORDF13

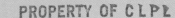

SUPERMAN® *FAMILY ADVENTURES*™

SUPER-PETS!

by Art Baltazar & Franco

SUPERMAN®
FAMILY ADVENTURES™

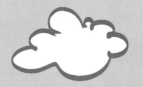

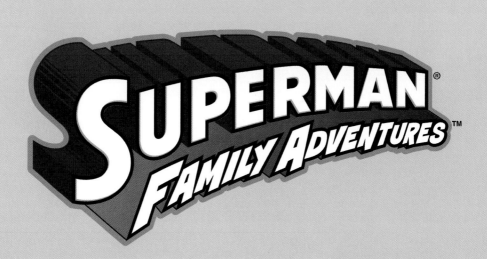

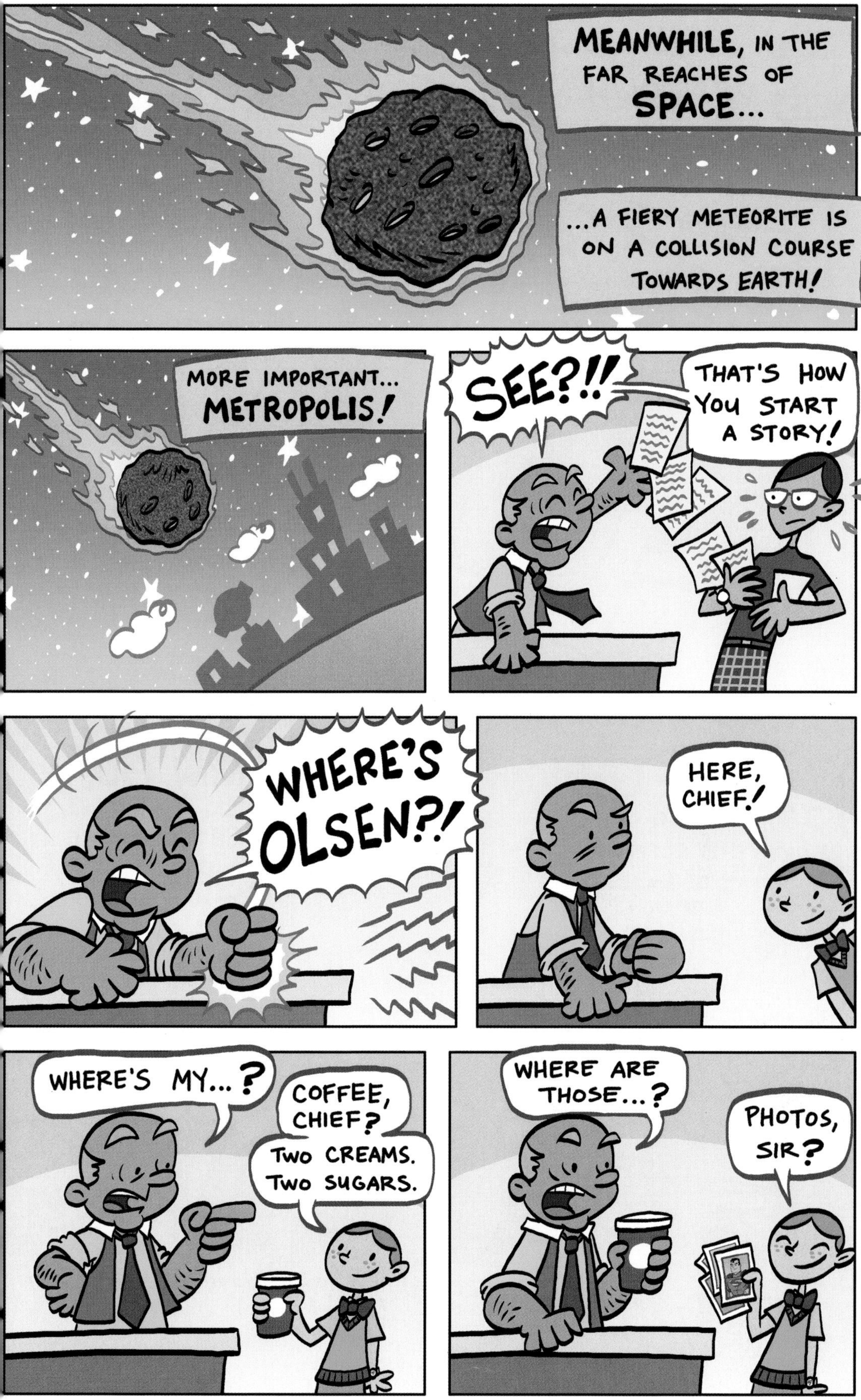
MEANWHILE, IN THE FAR REACHES OF SPACE...
...A FIERY METEORITE IS ON A COLLISION COURSE TOWARDS EARTH!
MORE IMPORTANT... METROPOLIS!
SEE?!!
THAT'S HOW YOU START A STORY!
WHERE'S OLSEN?!
HERE, CHIEF!
WHERE'S MY...?
COFFEE, CHIEF?
TWO CREAMS. TWO SUGARS.
WHERE ARE THOSE...?
PHOTOS, SIR?

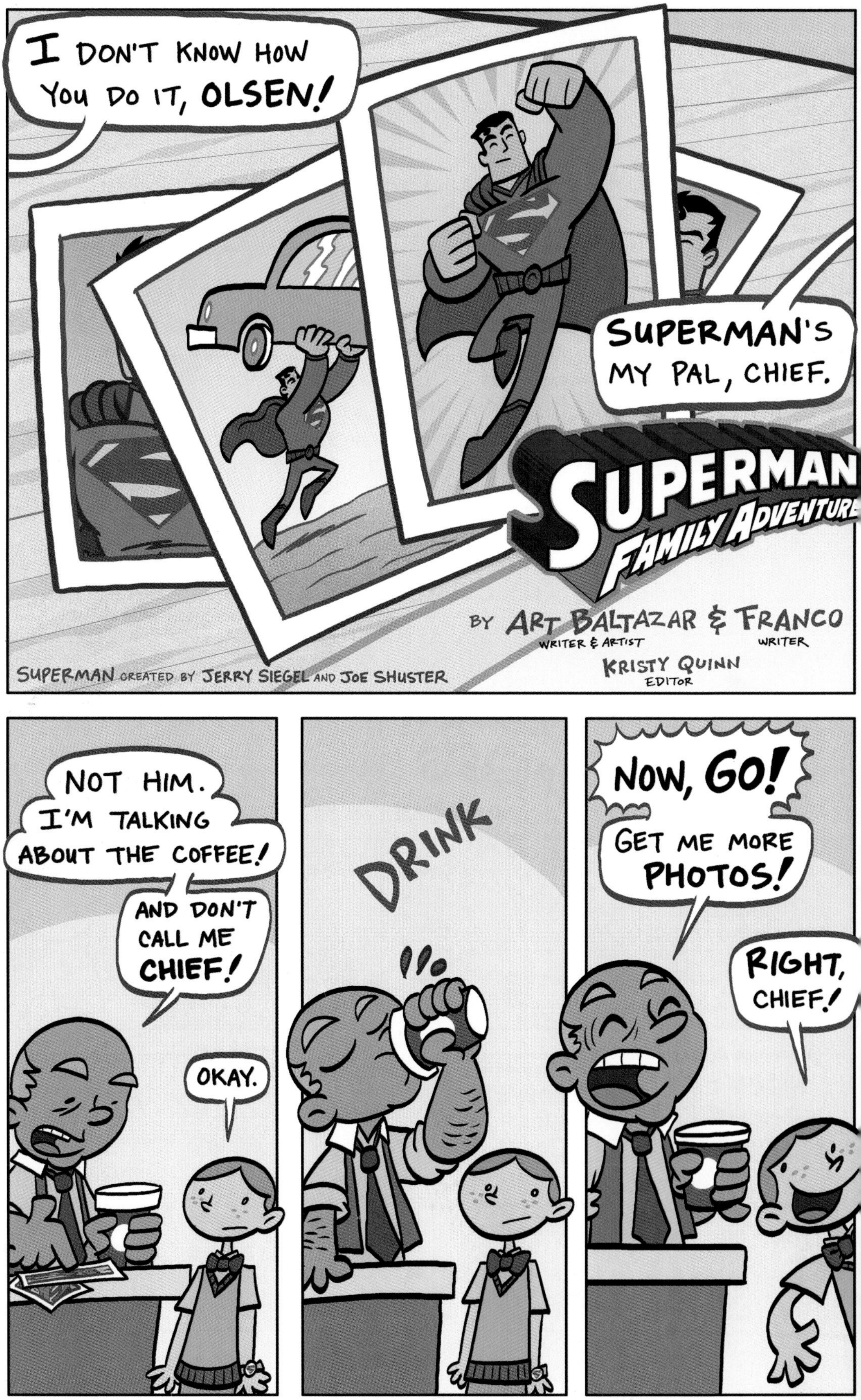

I DON'T KNOW HOW YOU DO IT, OLSEN!
SUPERMAN'S MY PAL, CHIEF.
SUPERMAN FAMILY ADVENTURES
BY ART BALTAZAR WRITER & ARTIST & FRANCO WRITER
KRISTY QUINN EDITOR
SUPERMAN CREATED BY JERRY SIEGEL AND JOE SHUSTER
NOT HIM. I'M TALKING ABOUT THE COFFEE!
AND DON'T CALL ME CHIEF!
OKAY.
DRINK
NOW, GO!
GET ME MORE PHOTOS!
RIGHT, CHIEF!

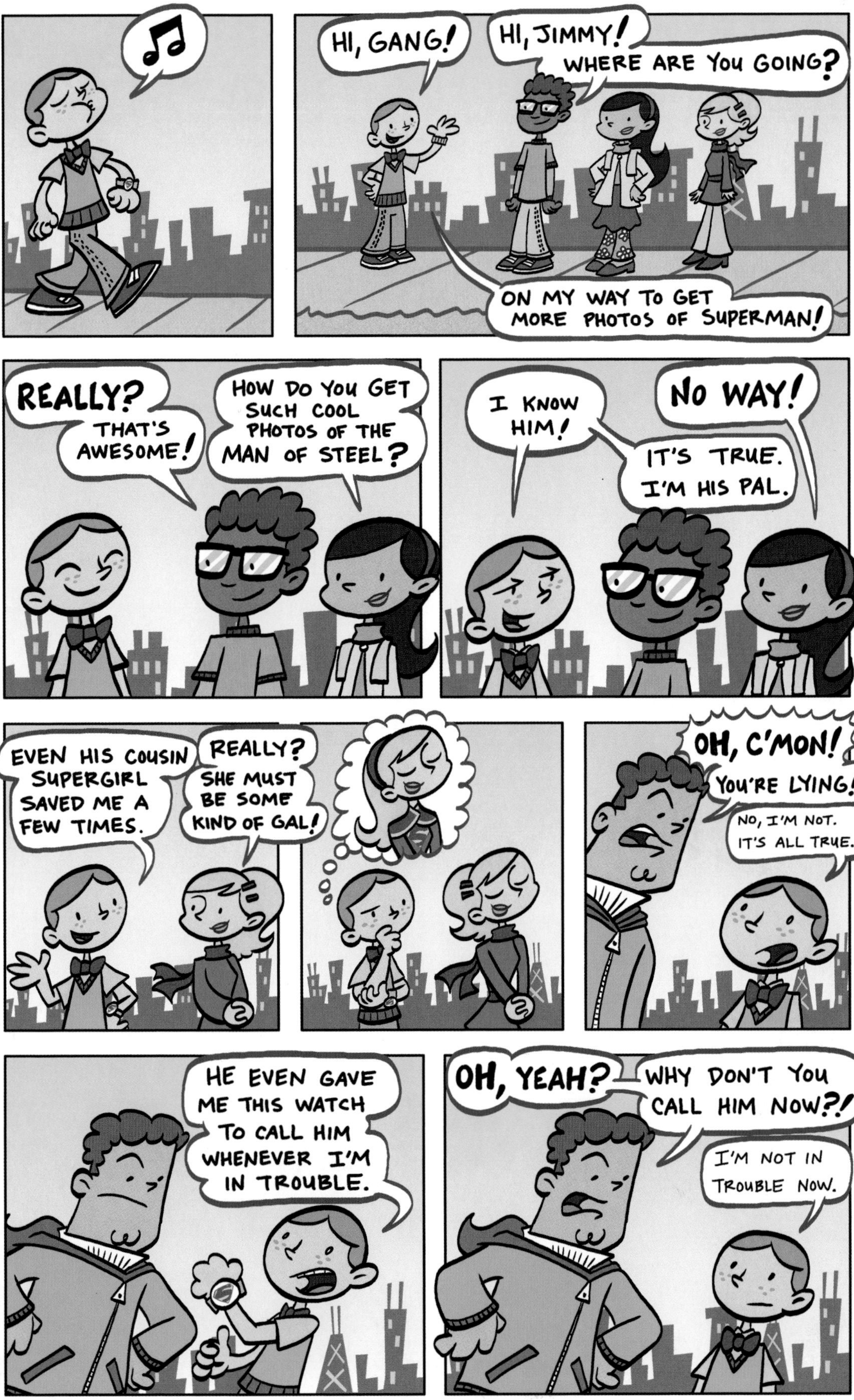
HI, GANG!
HI, JIMMY! WHERE ARE YOU GOING?
ON MY WAY TO GET MORE PHOTOS OF SUPERMAN!
REALLY? THAT'S AWESOME!
HOW DO YOU GET SUCH COOL PHOTOS OF THE MAN OF STEEL?
I KNOW HIM!
NO WAY!
IT'S TRUE. I'M HIS PAL.
EVEN HIS COUSIN SUPERGIRL SAVED ME A FEW TIMES.
REALLY? SHE MUST BE SOME KIND OF GAL!
OH, C'MON! YOU'RE LYING!
NO, I'M NOT. IT'S ALL TRUE.
HE EVEN GAVE ME THIS WATCH TO CALL HIM WHENEVER I'M IN TROUBLE.
OH, YEAH? WHY DON'T YOU CALL HIM NOW?!
I'M NOT IN TROUBLE NOW.

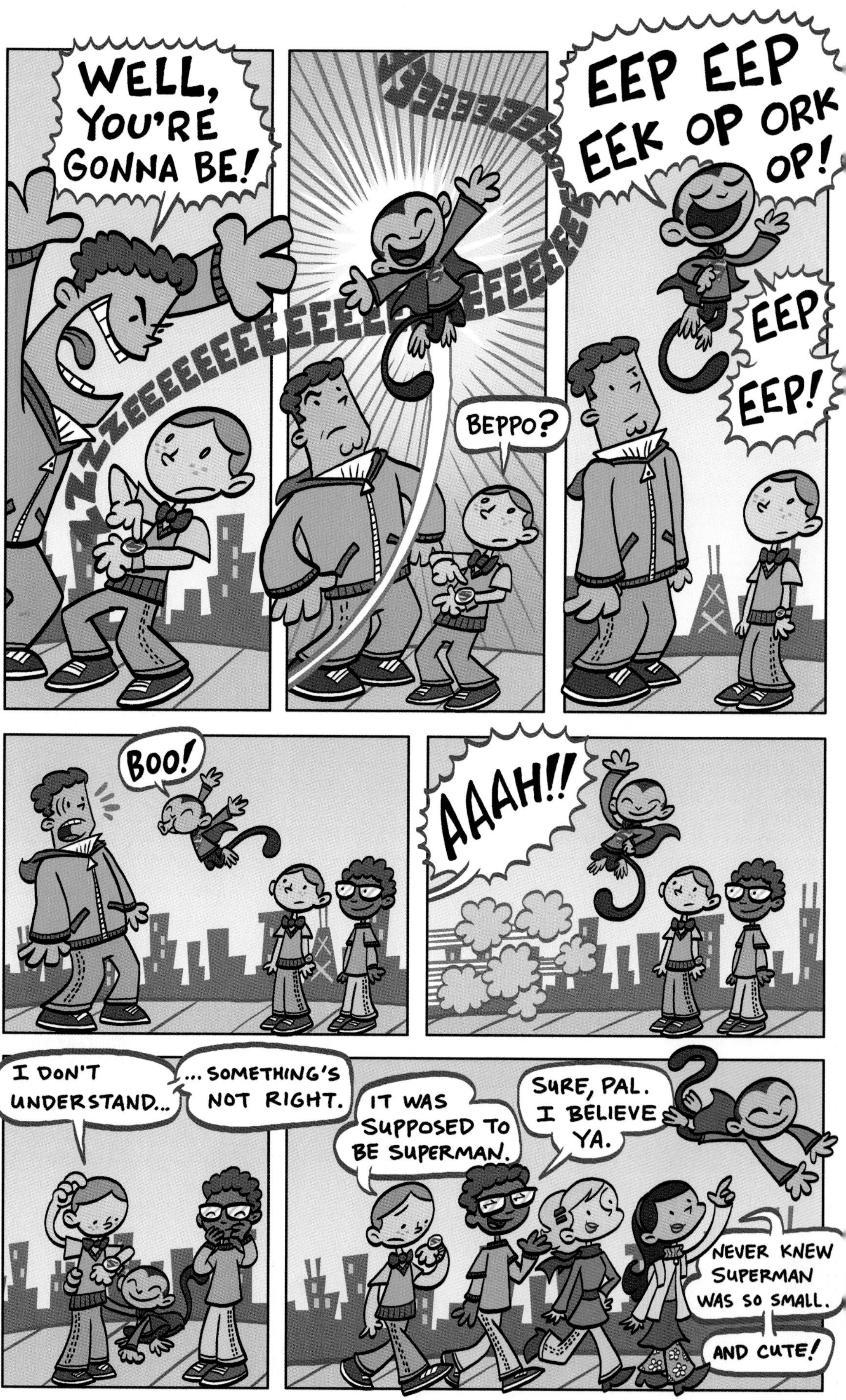
WELL, YOU'RE GONNA BE!
BEPPO?
EEP EEP EEK OP ORK OP!
EEP EEP!
BOO!
AAAH!!
I DON'T UNDERSTAND...
...SOMETHING'S NOT RIGHT.
IT WAS SUPPOSED TO BE SUPERMAN.
SURE, PAL. I BELIEVE YA.
NEVER KNEW SUPERMAN WAS SO SMALL.
AND CUTE!

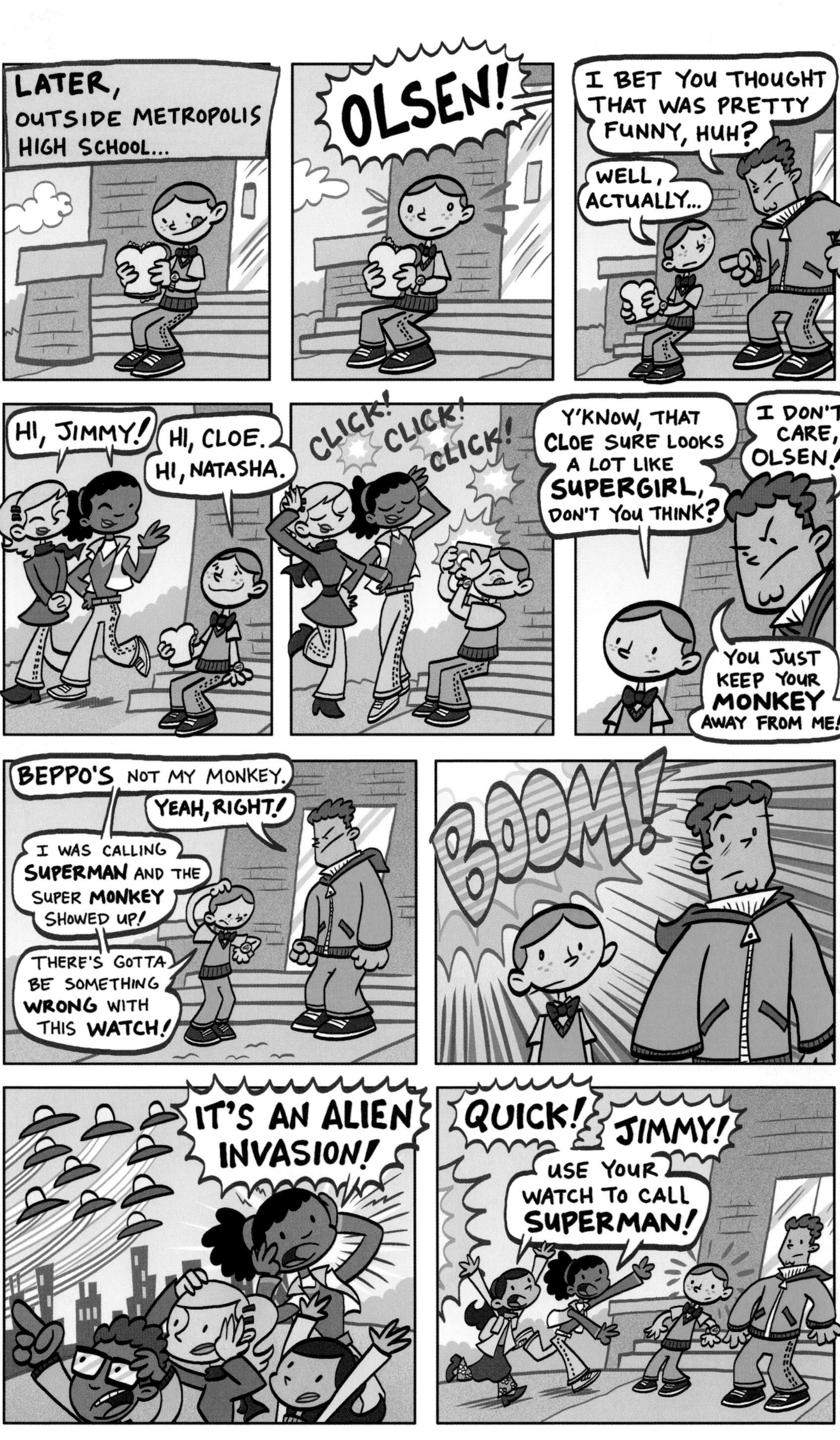
LATER, OUTSIDE METROPOLIS HIGH SCHOOL...
OLSEN!
I BET YOU THOUGHT THAT WAS PRETTY FUNNY, HUH?
WELL, ACTUALLY...
HI, JIMMY!
HI, CLOE. HI, NATASHA.
CLICK! CLICK! CLICK!
Y'KNOW, THAT CLOE SURE LOOKS A LOT LIKE SUPERGIRL, DON'T YOU THINK?
I DON'T CARE, OLSEN!
YOU JUST KEEP YOUR MONKEY AWAY FROM ME!
BEPPO'S NOT MY MONKEY.
YEAH, RIGHT!
I WAS CALLING SUPERMAN AND THE SUPER MONKEY SHOWED UP!
THERE'S GOTTA BE SOMETHING WRONG WITH THIS WATCH!
BOOM!
IT'S AN ALIEN INVASION!
QUICK!
JIMMY!
USE YOUR WATCH TO CALL SUPERMAN!

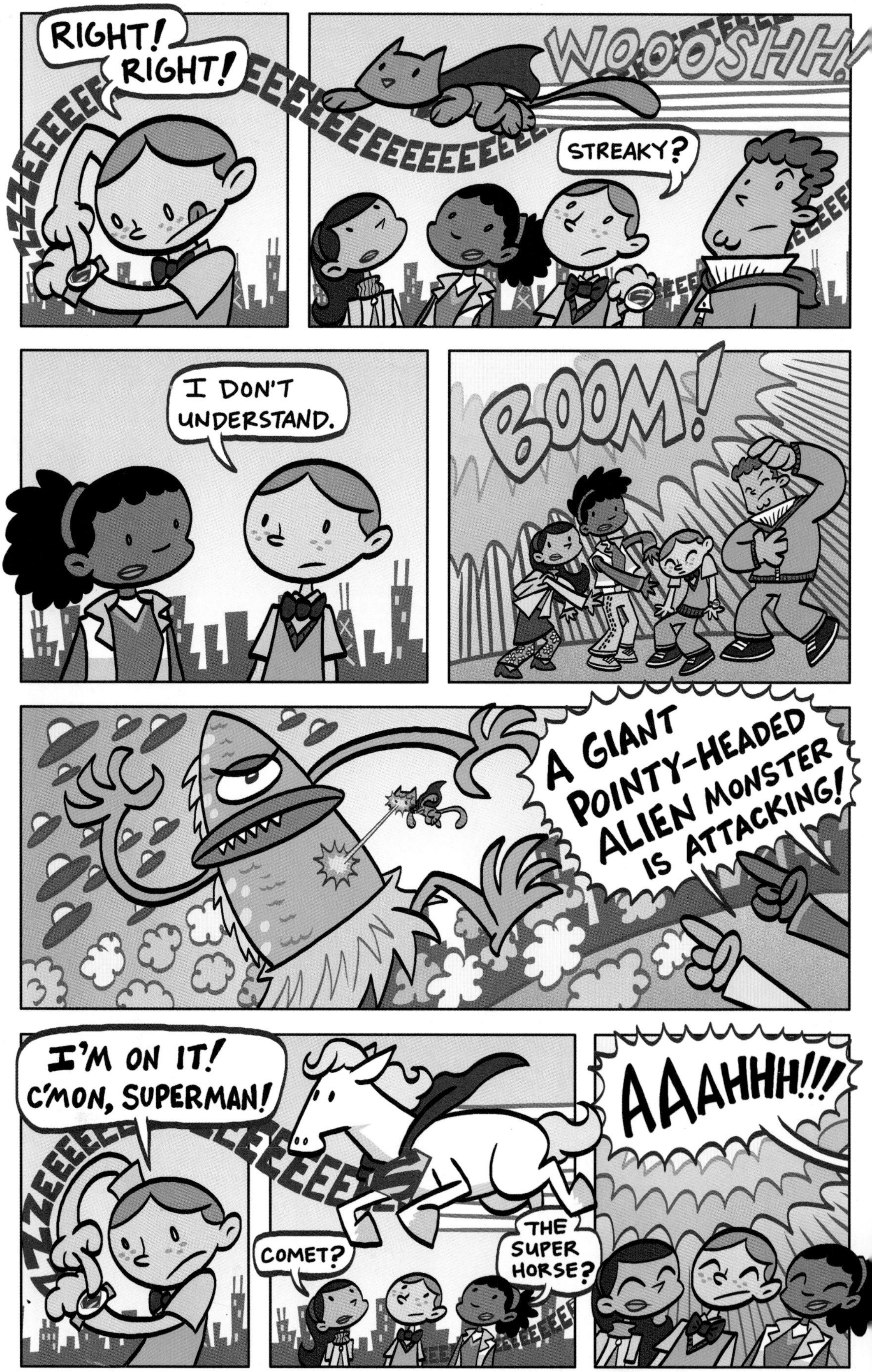
RIGHT! RIGHT!
ZZZEEEEEEEEEEEEEEEEEEEEEEE
WOOOSHH!
STREAKY?
I DON'T UNDERSTAND.
BOOM!
A GIANT POINTY-HEADED ALIEN MONSTER IS ATTACKING!
I'M ON IT! C'MON, SUPERMAN!
ZZZEEEEEEEEEEEE
COMET?
THE SUPER HORSE?
AAAHHH!!!

A GIANT SLIMY SIX-EYED ALIEN MONSTER WITH TENTACLES!

ZZZEEEEEEEE

KRYPTO?

ZZZEEEEEEEEEEEEE

HIYA, JIMMY!

FUZZY?

ZZEEEEEEEEEEEEEE

ZZZEEEEEEEEEEE

DON'T WORRY. THE WATCH IS WORKING.

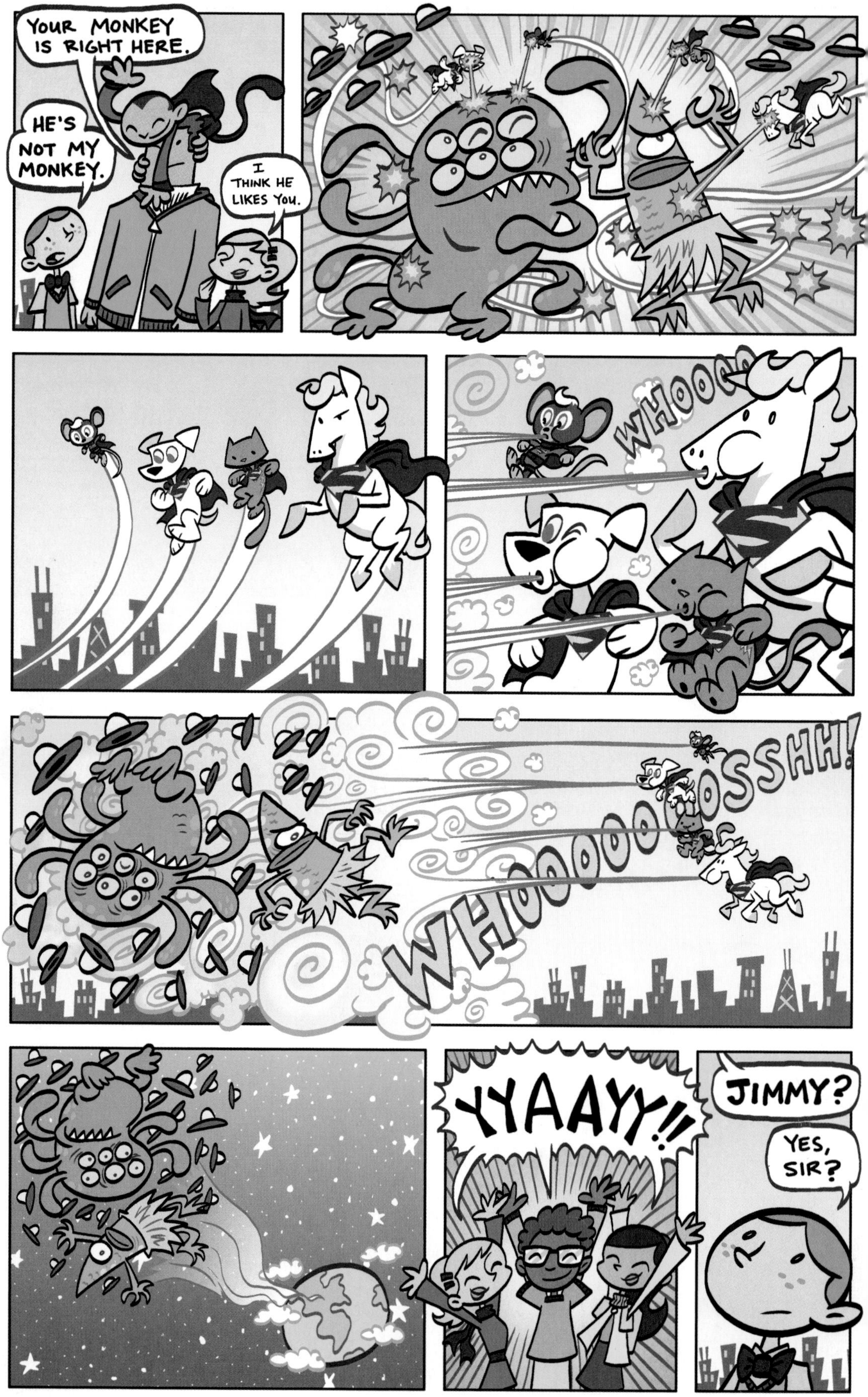
YOUR MONKEY IS RIGHT HERE.
HE'S NOT MY MONKEY.
I THINK HE LIKES YOU.
WHOOO
WHOOOOOOOOSSHH!
YYAAYY!!
JIMMY?
YES, SIR?

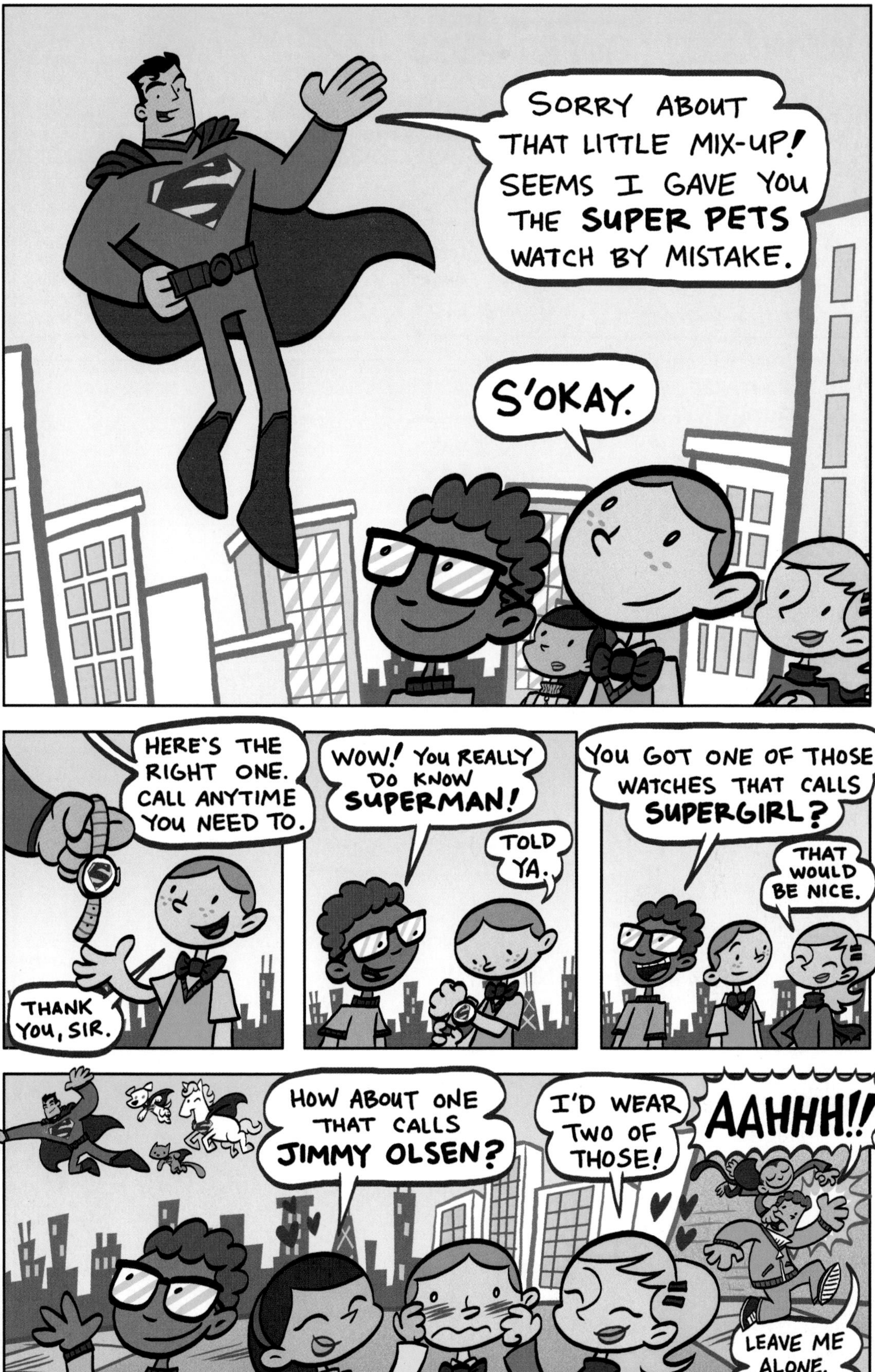
SORRY ABOUT THAT LITTLE MIX-UP! SEEMS I GAVE YOU THE SUPER PETS WATCH BY MISTAKE.
S'OKAY.
HERE'S THE RIGHT ONE. CALL ANYTIME YOU NEED TO.
THANK YOU, SIR.
WOW! YOU REALLY DO KNOW SUPERMAN!
TOLD YA.
YOU GOT ONE OF THOSE WATCHES THAT CALLS SUPERGIRL?
THAT WOULD BE NICE.
HOW ABOUT ONE THAT CALLS JIMMY OLSEN?
I'D WEAR TWO OF THOSE!
AAHHH!!
LEAVE ME ALONE, MONKEY!

—WHAT TIME IS IT?

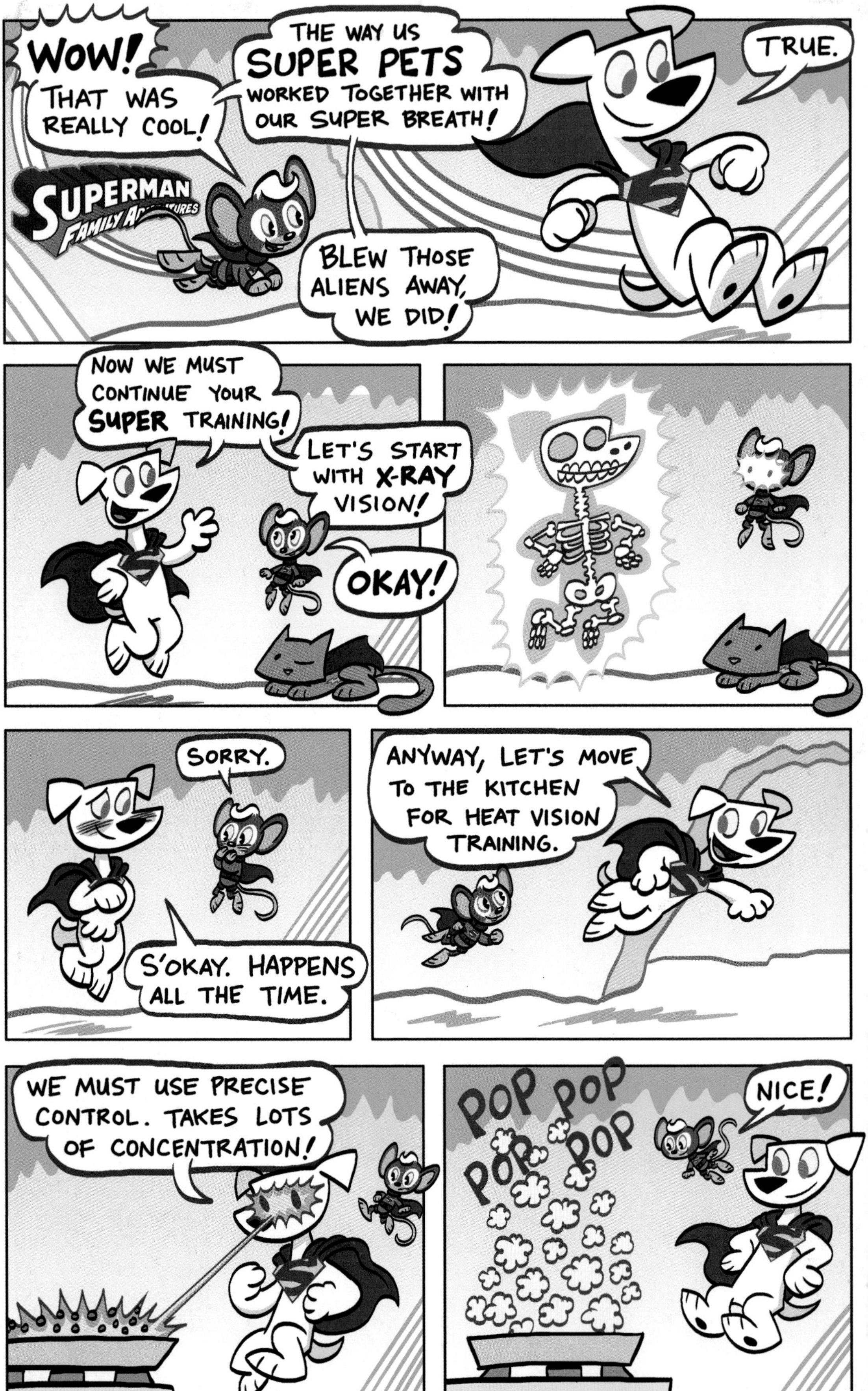

WOW! THAT WAS REALLY COOL!
SUPERMAN FAMILY ADVENTURES
THE WAY US SUPER PETS WORKED TOGETHER WITH OUR SUPER BREATH!
BLEW THOSE ALIENS AWAY, WE DID!
TRUE.
NOW WE MUST CONTINUE YOUR SUPER TRAINING!
LET'S START WITH X-RAY VISION!
OKAY!
SORRY.
S'OKAY. HAPPENS ALL THE TIME.
ANYWAY, LET'S MOVE TO THE KITCHEN FOR HEAT VISION TRAINING.
WE MUST USE PRECISE CONTROL. TAKES LOTS OF CONCENTRATION!
POP POP POP POP
NICE!

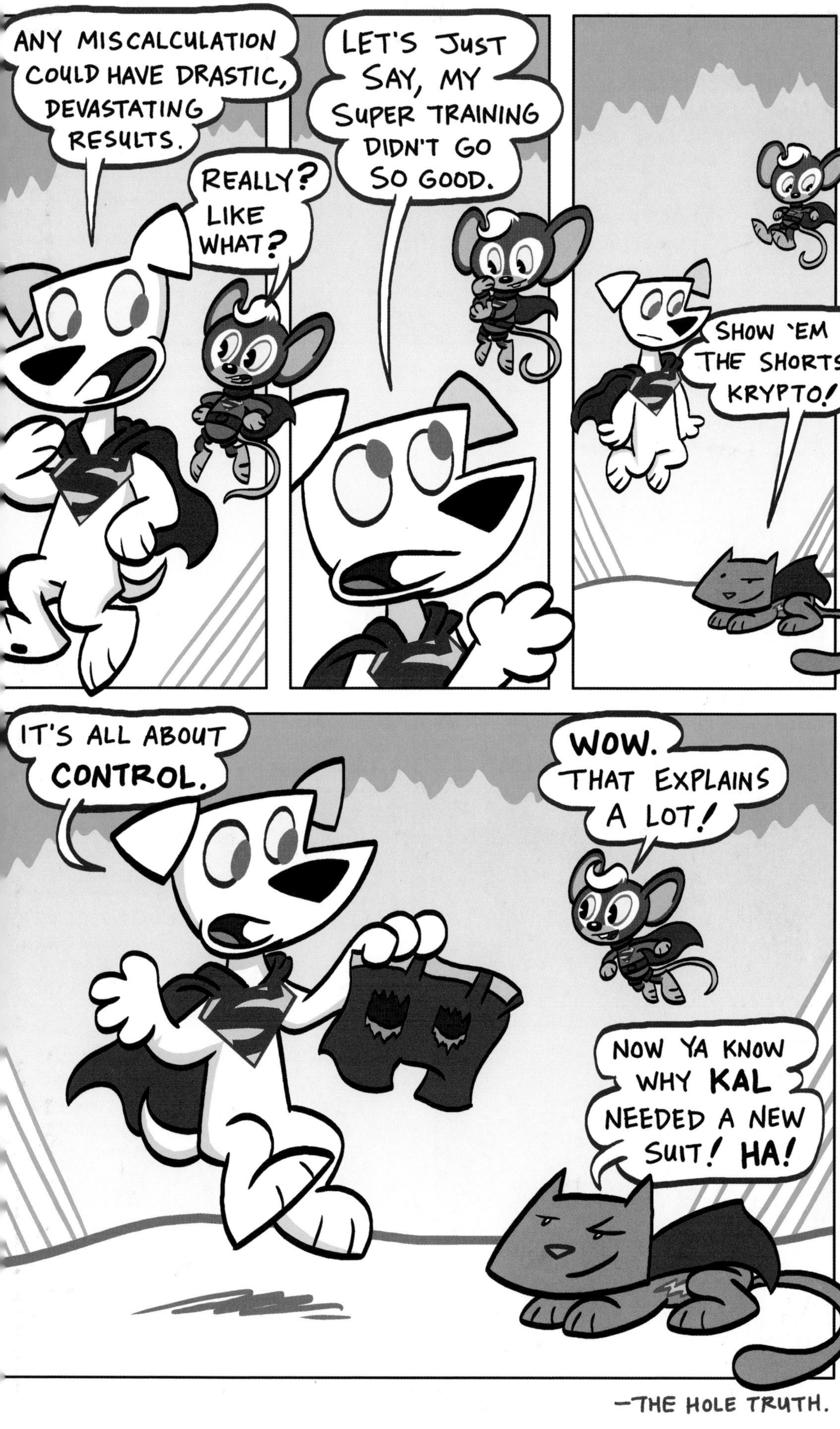
ANY MISCALCULATION COULD HAVE DRASTIC, DEVASTATING RESULTS.
REALLY? LIKE WHAT?
LET'S JUST SAY, MY SUPER TRAINING DIDN'T GO SO GOOD.
SHOW 'EM THE SHORTS, KRYPTO!
IT'S ALL ABOUT **CONTROL**.
WOW. THAT EXPLAINS A LOT!
NOW YA KNOW WHY **KAL** NEEDED A NEW SUIT! **HA!**

—THE HOLE TRUTH.

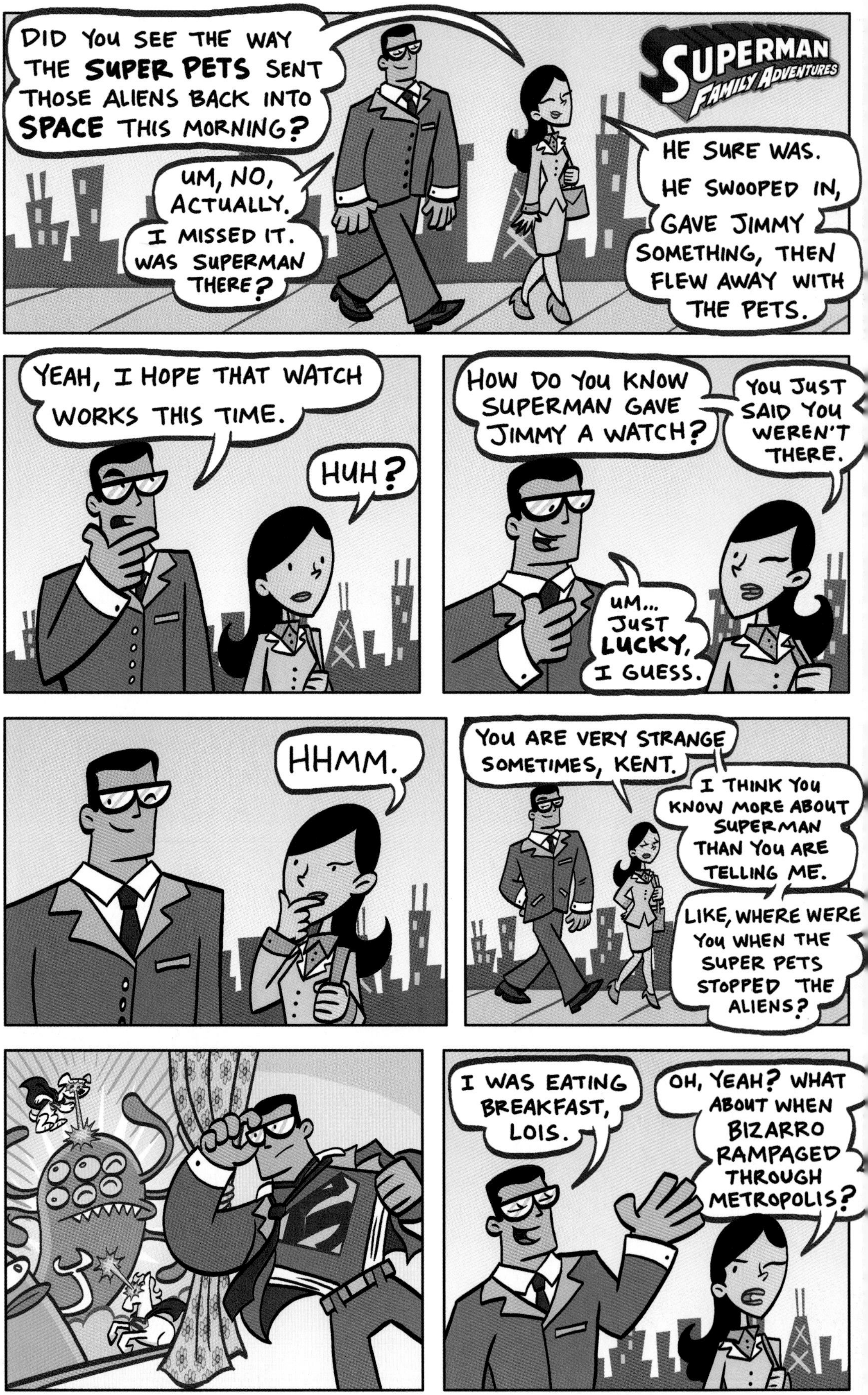
DID YOU SEE THE WAY THE SUPER PETS SENT THOSE ALIENS BACK INTO SPACE THIS MORNING?
SUPERMAN FAMILY ADVENTURES
UM, NO, ACTUALLY. I MISSED IT. WAS SUPERMAN THERE?
HE SURE WAS. HE SWOOPED IN, GAVE JIMMY SOMETHING, THEN FLEW AWAY WITH THE PETS.
YEAH, I HOPE THAT WATCH WORKS THIS TIME.
HUH?
HOW DO YOU KNOW SUPERMAN GAVE JIMMY A WATCH?
YOU JUST SAID YOU WEREN'T THERE.
UM... JUST LUCKY, I GUESS.
HHMM.
YOU ARE VERY STRANGE SOMETIMES, KENT.
I THINK YOU KNOW MORE ABOUT SUPERMAN THAN YOU ARE TELLING ME.
LIKE, WHERE WERE YOU WHEN THE SUPER PETS STOPPED THE ALIENS?
I WAS EATING BREAKFAST, LOIS.
OH, YEAH? WHAT ABOUT WHEN BIZARRO RAMPAGED THROUGH METROPOLIS?

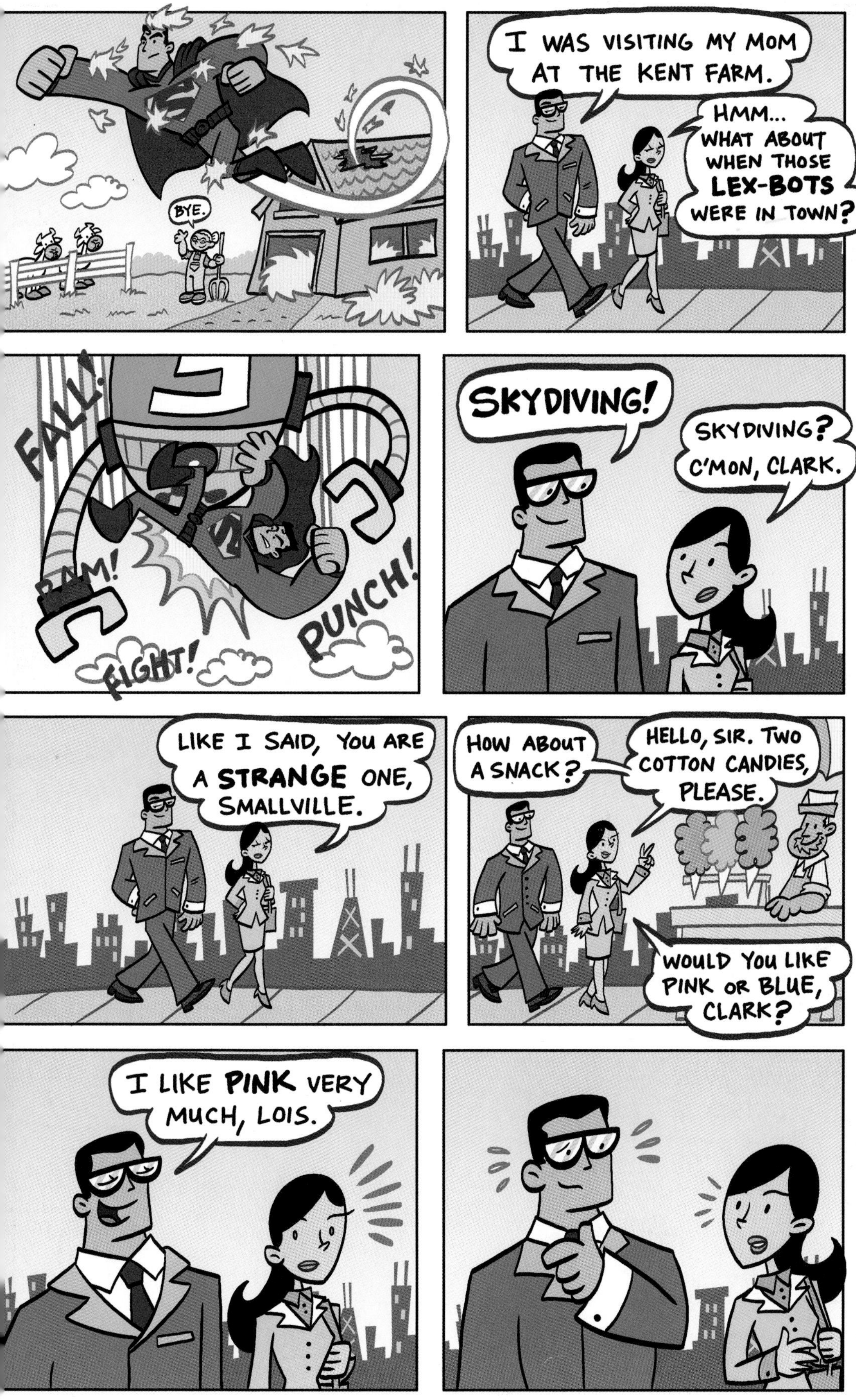
BYE.
I WAS VISITING MY MOM AT THE KENT FARM.
HMM... WHAT ABOUT WHEN THOSE LEX-BOTS WERE IN TOWN?
FALL!
BAM!
PUNCH!
FIGHT!
SKYDIVING!
SKYDIVING? C'MON, CLARK.
LIKE I SAID, YOU ARE A STRANGE ONE, SMALLVILLE.
HOW ABOUT A SNACK?
HELLO, SIR. TWO COTTON CANDIES, PLEASE.
WOULD YOU LIKE PINK OR BLUE, CLARK?
I LIKE PINK VERY MUCH, LOIS.

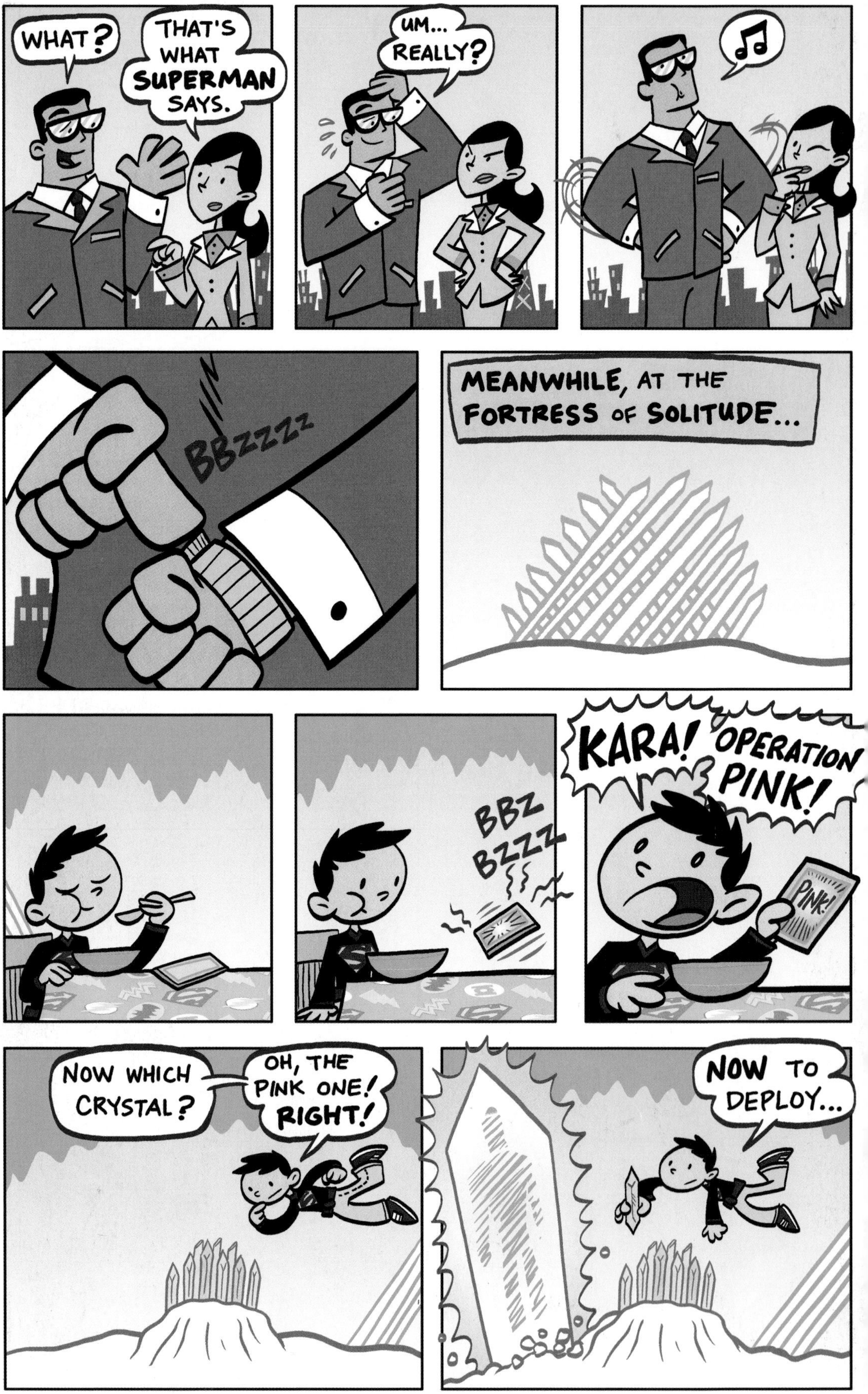
WHAT?
THAT'S WHAT SUPERMAN SAYS.
UM... REALLY?
♫
BBZZZZ
MEANWHILE, AT THE FORTRESS OF SOLITUDE...
BBZ BZZZ
KARA! OPERATION PINK!
PINK!
NOW WHICH CRYSTAL?
OH, THE PINK ONE! RIGHT!
NOW TO DEPLOY...

... THE SUPERMAN ROBOT!

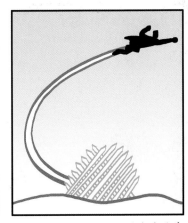

WHAT HAPPENED HERE?

OPERATION PINK!

OH, IT'S THE PINK CRYSTAL.

KARA! WAIT! NO!

BMMMM!

UH, OH. NOW THERE ARE TWO OF THEM HEADING TO METROPOLIS.

UM... NOT GOOD.

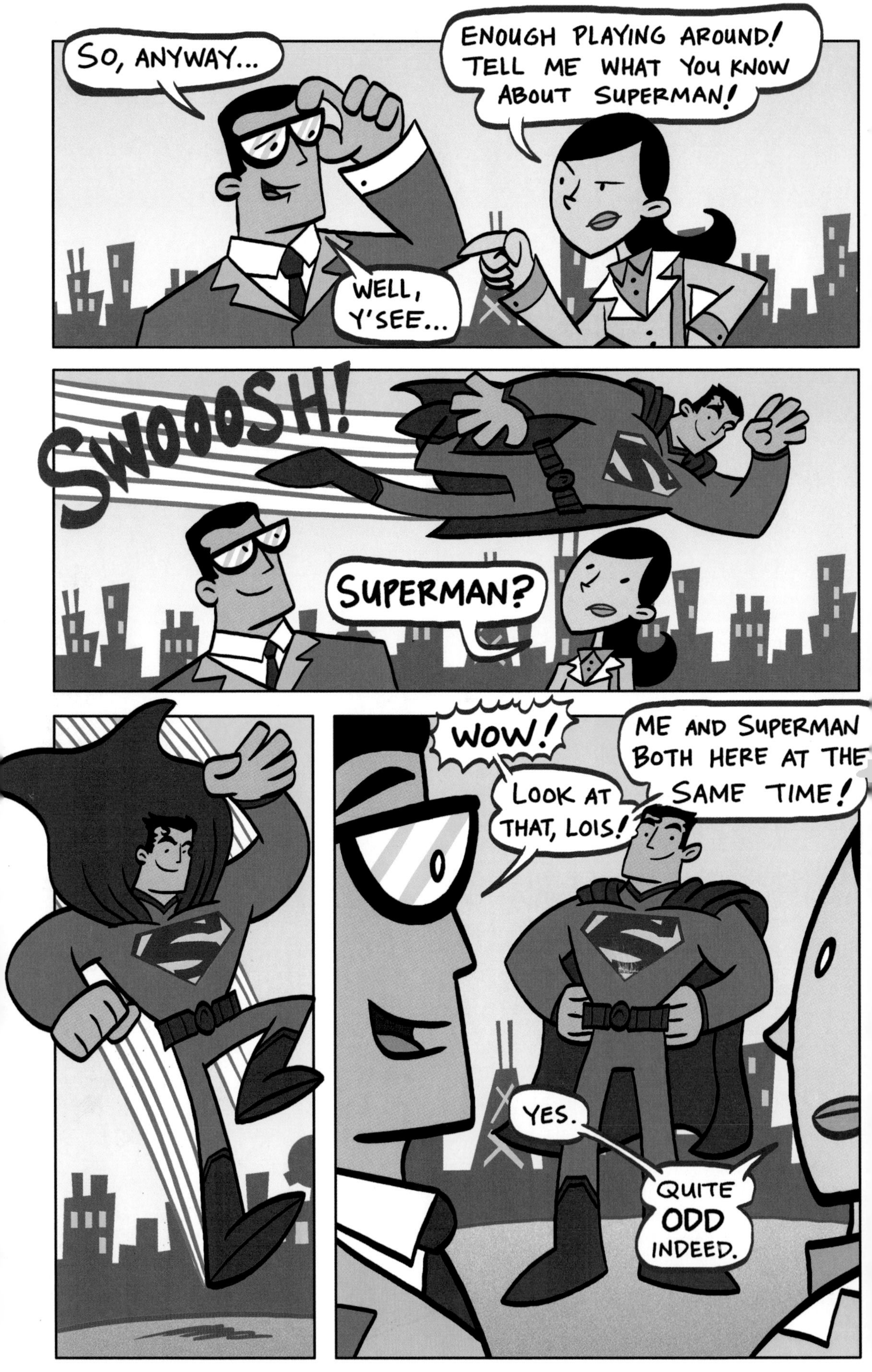

SO, ANYWAY...
ENOUGH PLAYING AROUND! TELL ME WHAT YOU KNOW ABOUT SUPERMAN!
WELL, Y'SEE...
SWOOOSH!
SUPERMAN?
WOW!
LOOK AT THAT, LOIS!
ME AND SUPERMAN BOTH HERE AT THE SAME TIME!
YES.
QUITE ODD INDEED.

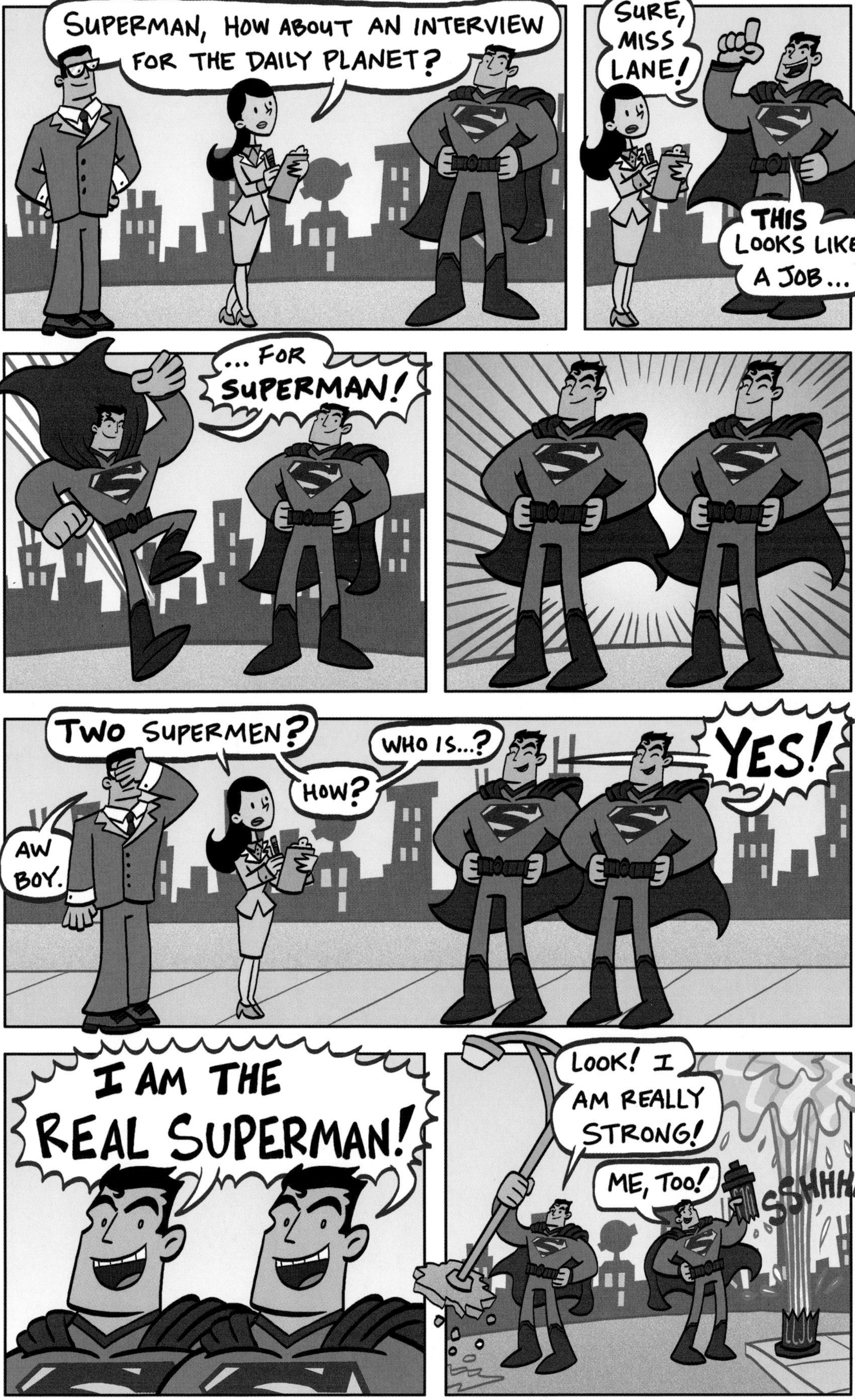
SUPERMAN, HOW ABOUT AN INTERVIEW FOR THE DAILY PLANET?
SURE, MISS LANE!
THIS LOOKS LIKE A JOB...
... FOR SUPERMAN!
TWO SUPERMEN?
HOW?
WHO IS...?
YES!
AW BOY.
I AM THE REAL SUPERMAN!
LOOK! I AM REALLY STRONG!
ME, TOO!
SSHHHH

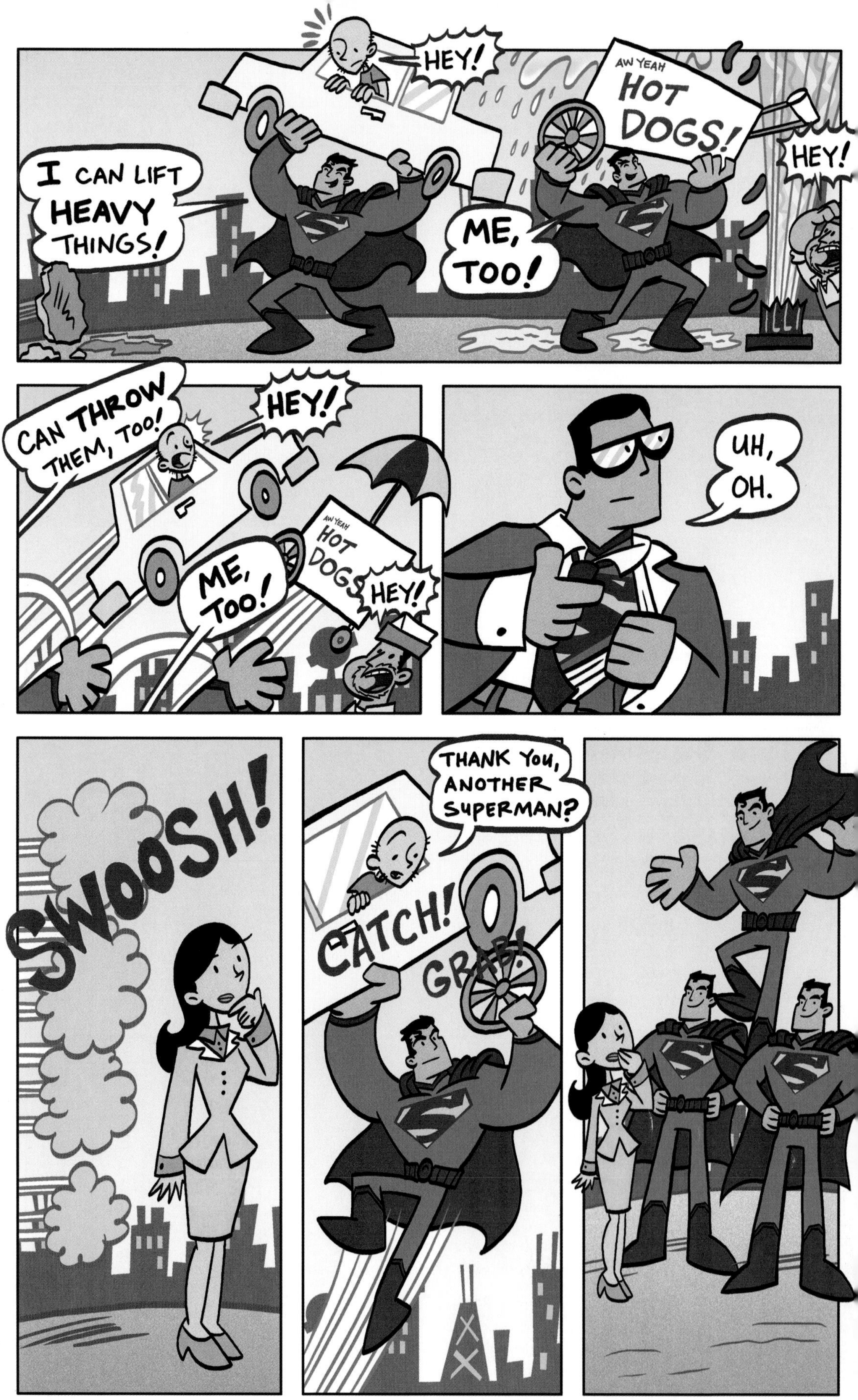
HEY!
AW YEAH
HOT DOGS!
I CAN LIFT HEAVY THINGS!
ME, TOO!
HEY!
CAN THROW THEM, TOO!
HEY!
AW YEAH
HOT DOGS
ME, TOO!
HEY!
UH, OH.
SWOOSH!
THANK YOU, ANOTHER SUPERMAN?
CATCH!
GRAB!

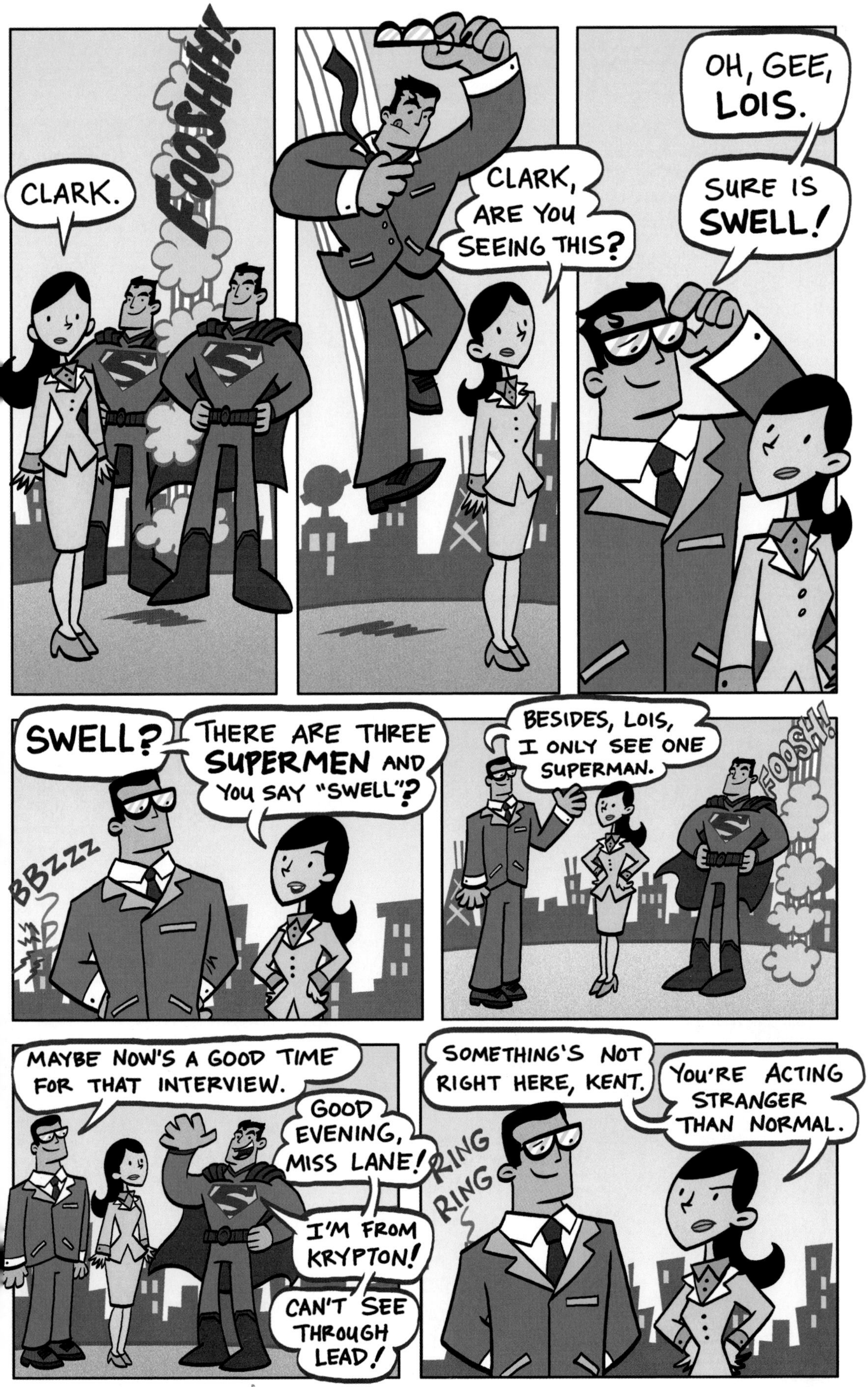
CLARK.
FOOSHH!
CLARK, ARE YOU SEEING THIS?
OH, GEE, LOIS.
SURE IS SWELL!
SWELL?
THERE ARE THREE SUPERMEN AND YOU SAY "SWELL"?
BBZZZZ
BESIDES, LOIS, I ONLY SEE ONE SUPERMAN.
FOOSH!
MAYBE NOW'S A GOOD TIME FOR THAT INTERVIEW.
GOOD EVENING, MISS LANE!
I'M FROM KRYPTON!
CAN'T SEE THROUGH LEAD!
SOMETHING'S NOT RIGHT HERE, KENT.
YOU'RE ACTING STRANGER THAN NORMAL.
RING RING

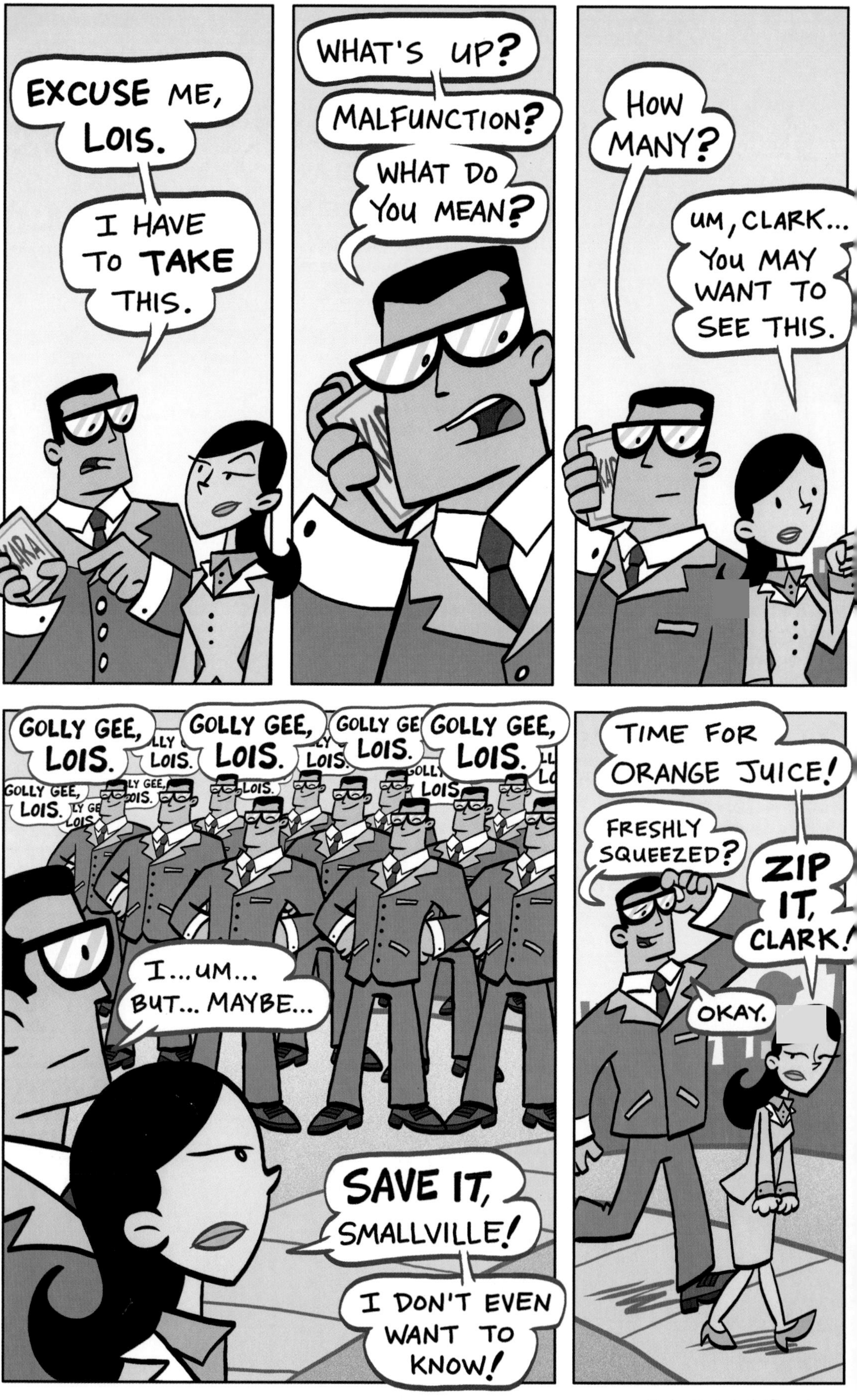

EXCUSE ME, LOIS.
I HAVE TO TAKE THIS.
KARA
WHAT'S UP?
MALFUNCTION?
WHAT DO YOU MEAN?
HOW MANY?
UM, CLARK... YOU MAY WANT TO SEE THIS.
GOLLY GEE, LOIS.
GOLLY GEE, LOIS.
GOLLY GEE, LOIS.
GOLLY GEE, LOIS.
I... UM... BUT... MAYBE...
SAVE IT, SMALLVILLE!
I DON'T EVEN WANT TO KNOW!
TIME FOR ORANGE JUICE!
FRESHLY SQUEEZED?
ZIP IT, CLARK!
OKAY.

–SILENCE? YES.

SUPERMAN®

FAMILY ADVENTURES™

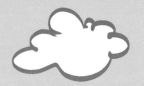

CREATORS

ART BALTAZAR IS A CARTOONIST MACHINE FROM THE HEART OF CHICAGO! HE DEFINES CARTOONS AND COMICS NOT ONLY AS AN ART STYLE, BUT AS A WAY OF LIFE. CURRENTLY, ART IS THE CREATIVE FORCE BEHIND THE NEW YORK TIMES BEST-SELLING, EISNER AWARD-WINNING, DC COMICS SERIES TINY TITANS, AND THE CO-WRITER FOR BILLY BATSON AND THE MAGIC OF SHAZAM! AND CO-CREATOR OF SUPERMAN FAMILY ADVENTURES. ART IS LIVING THE DREAM! HE DRAWS COMICS AND NEVER HAS TO LEAVE THE HOUSE. HE LIVES WITH HIS LOVELY WIFE, ROSE, BIG BOY SONNY, LITTLE BOY GORDON, AND LITTLE GIRL AUDREY. RIGHT ON!

ART BALTAZAR

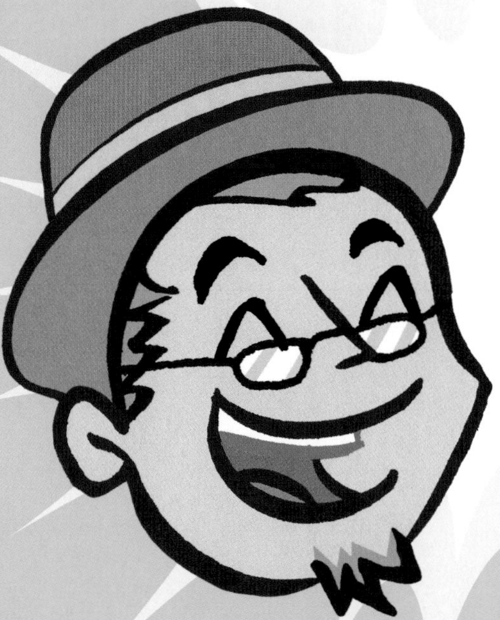

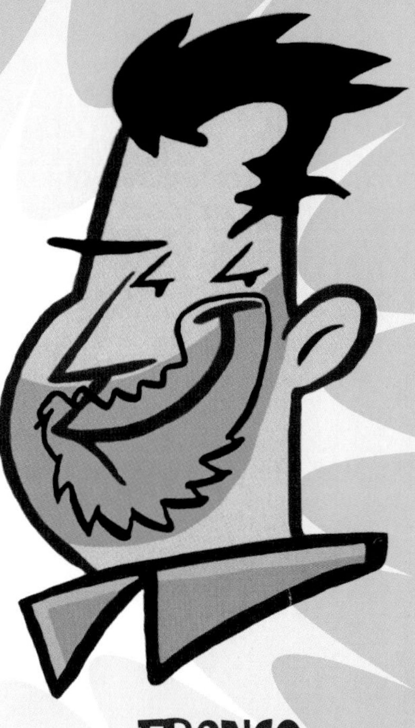

FRANCO

FRANCO AURELIANI, BRONX, NEW YORK BORN WRITER AND ARTIST, HAS BEEN DRAWING COMICS SINCE HE COULD HOLD A CRAYON. CURRENTLY RESIDING IN UPSTATE NEW YORK WITH HIS WIFE, IVETTE, AND SON, NICOLAS, FRANCO SPENDS MOST OF HIS DAYS IN A BATCAVE-LIKE STUDIO WHERE HE PRODUCES DC'S TINY TITANS COMICS. IN 1995, FRANCO FOUNDED BLINDWOLF STUDIOS, AN INDEPENDENT ART STUDIO WHERE HE AND FELLOW CREATORS CAN CREATE CHILDREN'S COMICS. FRANCO IS THE CREATOR, ARTIST, AND WRITER OF WEIRDSVILLE, L'IL CREEPS, AND EAGLE ALL STAR, AS WELL AS THE CO-CREATOR AND WRITER OF PATRICK THE WOLF BOY. WHEN HE'S NOT WRITING AND DRAWING, FRANCO ALSO TEACHES HIGH SCHOOL ART.

GLOSSARY

collision (kuh-LIZH-uhn)—the act or instance of crashing together forcefully, often at high speeds

concentration (KON-suhn-tray-shuhn)—the act of focusing your thoughts and attention on something

deploy (DEE-ploi)—to move, spread out, or place in position for some purpose

devastating (DEV-uh-stay-ting)—reducing to ruin, or destroying

fortress (FOR-triss)—a place that is strengthened against attack

invasion (in-VAY-zhun)—the act of entering for conquest or plunder

lead (LED)—a soft, gray metal

malfunction (mal-FUNG-shuhn)— to fail to operate properly

meteorite (MEE-tee-ur-rite)—a remaining part of a meteor that falls to Earth before it has burned up

miscalculation (mis-KAL-kyoo-lay-shuhn)— a mistake made in estimating

precise (pri-SISE)—very accurate or exact

rampaged (RAM-payjd)—rushing around in a noisy, destructive way

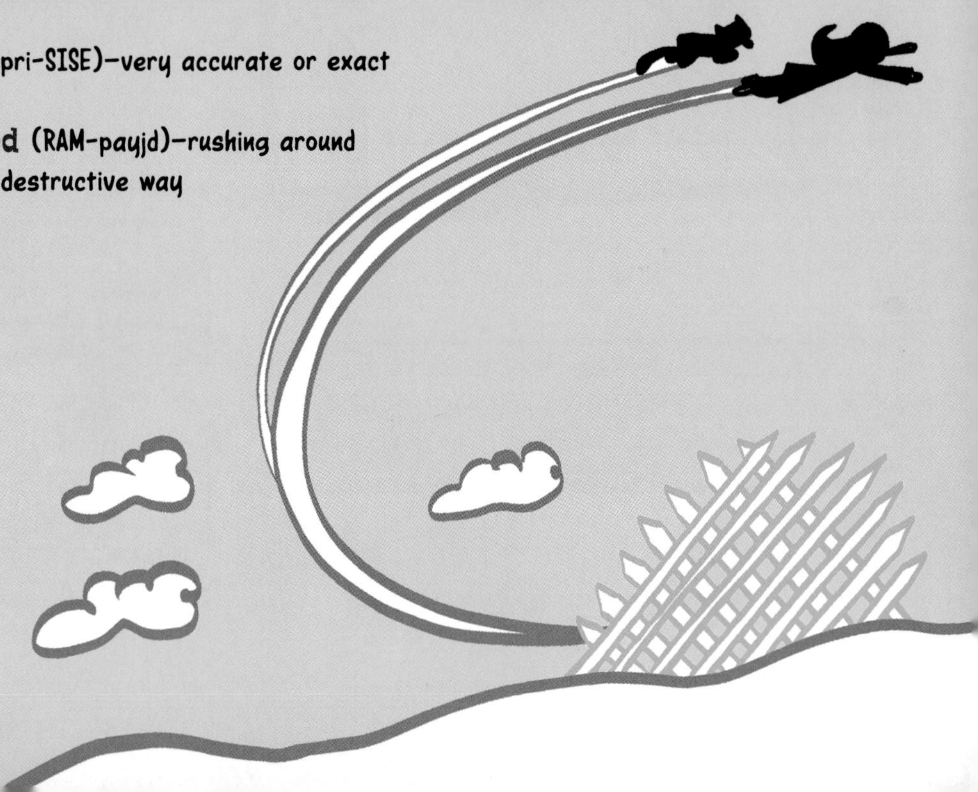

VISUAL QUESTIONS & PROMPTS

1. CLARK KENT IS SECRETLY SUPERMAN. WHY DO YOU THINK HE KEEPS THIS SECRET FROM LOIS LANE AND OTHER EARTHLINGS?

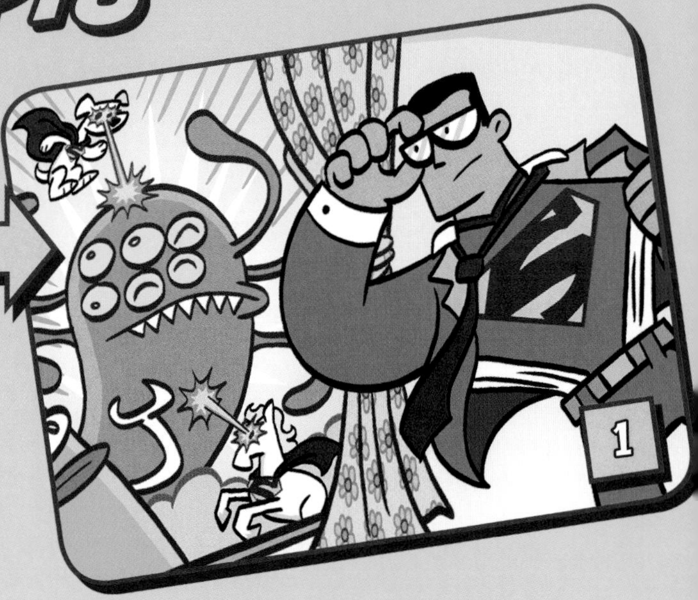
1

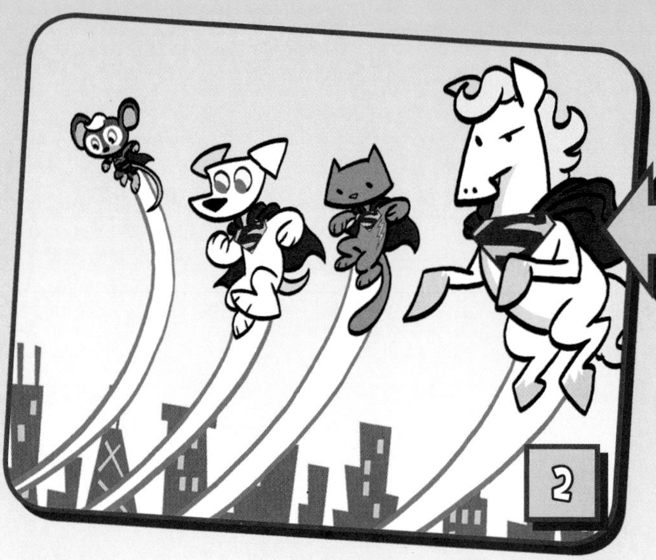
2

2. SUPERMAN HAS MANY SUPER-PETS! WHICH SUPER-PET IS YOUR FAVORITE, AND WHY?

3. JIMMY OLSEN HAS A WATCH THAT CAN SIGNAL SUPERMAN. THINK OF AT LEAST TWO TIMES IN YOUR LIFE YOU WOULD HAVE SIGNALED THE MAN OF STEEL IF YOU HAD THIS WATCH. WRITE DOWN YOUR ANSWERS.

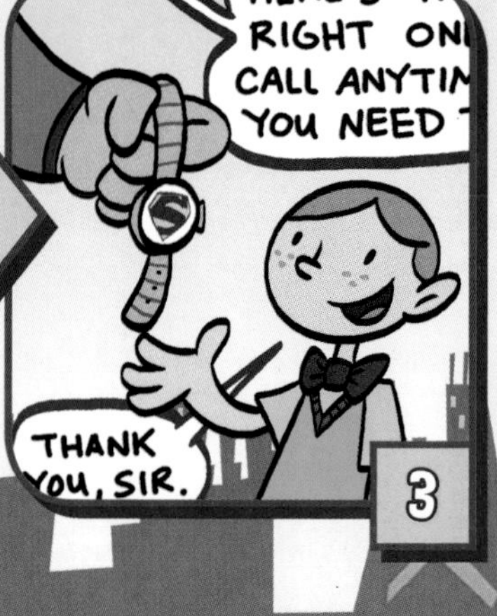
HERE'S
RIGHT
CALL
YOU NEED
THANK YOU, SIR.
3

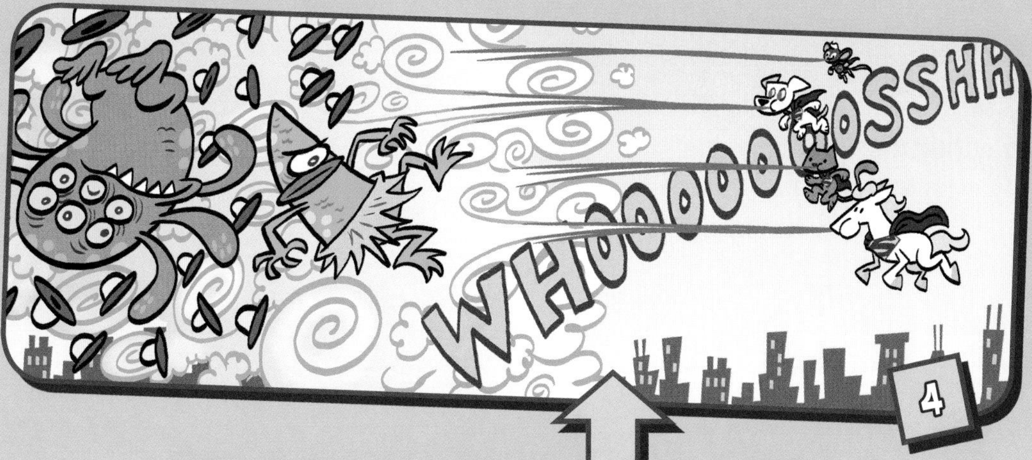
WHOOOOOOOSSHH
4

4. THE SUPER-PETS WORK TOGETHER TO DEFEAT THE ALIEN INVADERS. DO YOU THINK ANY OF THEM COULD HAVE HANDLED THE SITUATION ALONE?

5. WRITE YOUR OWN SUPERMAN FAMILY ADVENTURE! WHO WILL SUPERMAN AND HIS SUPER-PETS BATTLE AGAINST IN YOUR STORY?

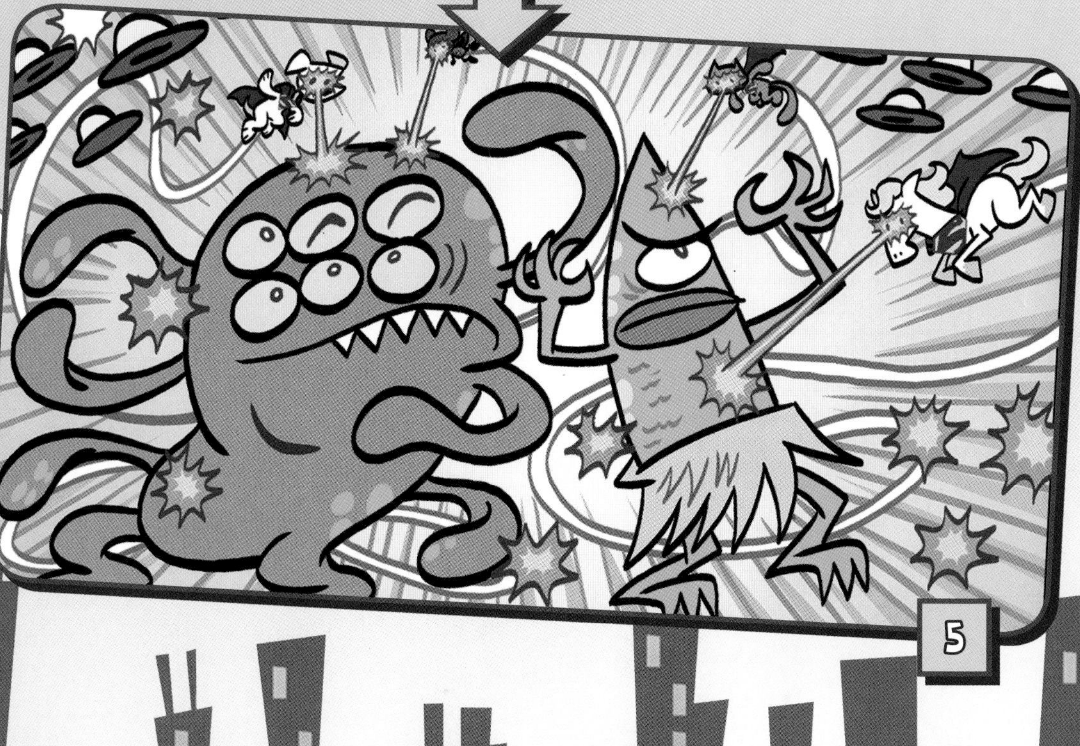
5

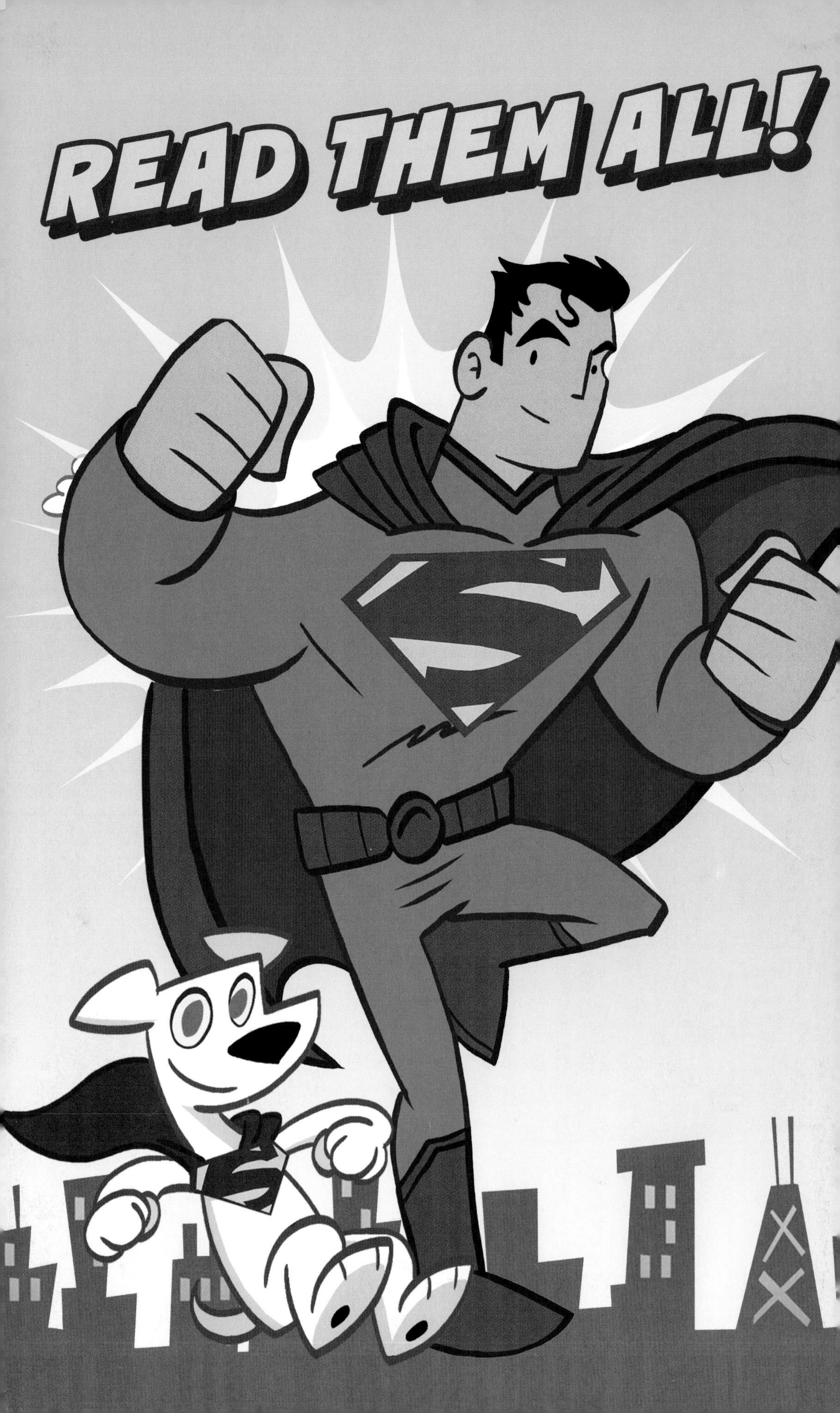
READ THEM ALL!

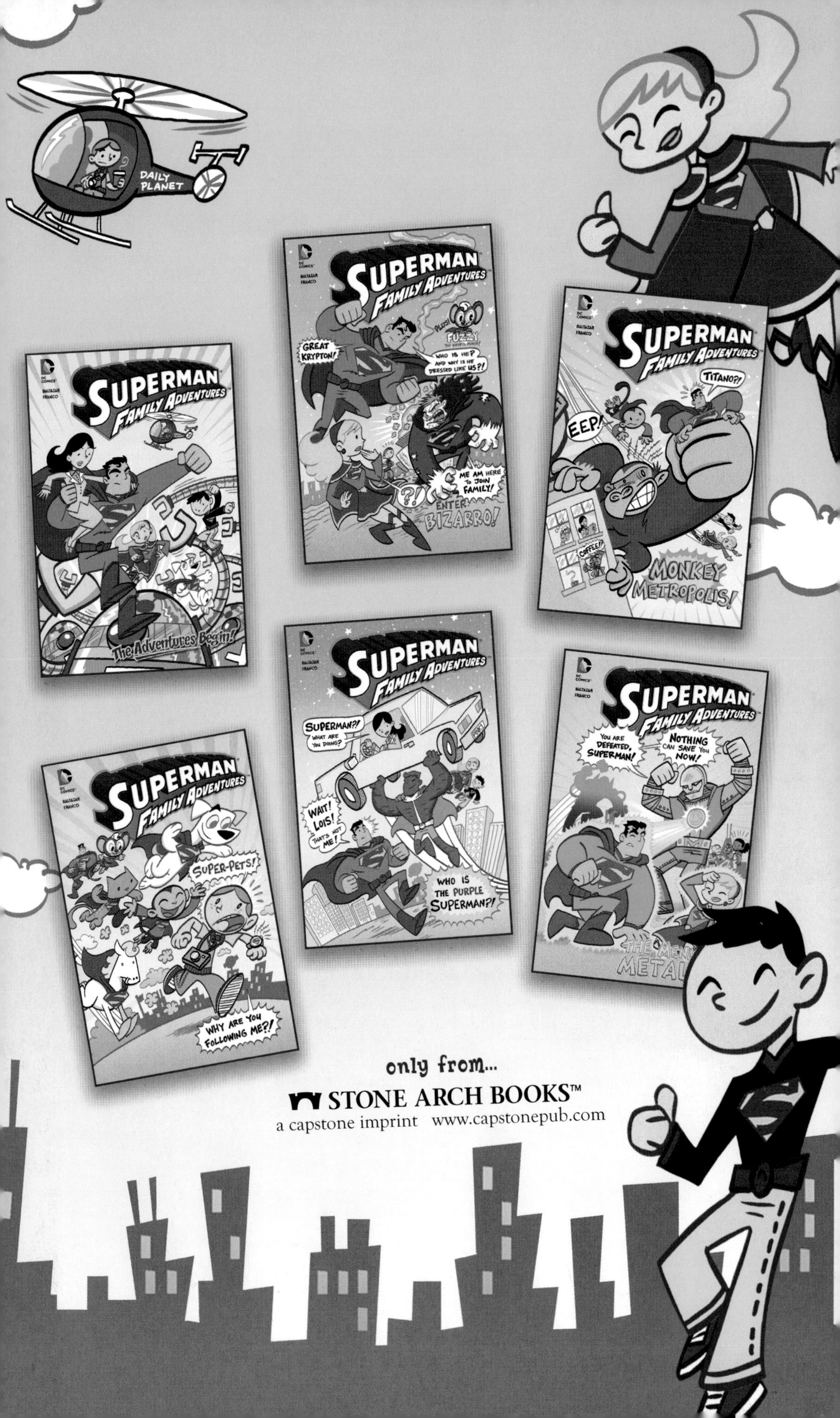
DAILY PLANET
SUPERMAN FAMILY ADVENTURES
BALTAZAR FRANCO
GREAT KRYPTON!
WHO IS HE? AND WHY IS HE DRESSED LIKE US?!
FUZZY
ME AM HERE TO JOIN FAMILY!
?!
ENTER: BIZARRO!
SUPERMAN FAMILY ADVENTURES
BALTAZAR FRANCO
The Adventures Begin!
SUPERMAN FAMILY ADVENTURES
BALTAZAR FRANCO
TITANO?!
EEP!
COFFEE!?
MONKEY METROPOLIS!
SUPERMAN FAMILY ADVENTURES
BALTAZAR FRANCO
SUPERMAN?! WHAT ARE YOU DOING?
WAIT! LOIS! THAT'S NOT ME!
WHO IS THE PURPLE SUPERMAN?!
SUPERMAN FAMILY ADVENTURES
BALTAZAR FRANCO
YOU ARE DEFEATED, SUPERMAN!
NOTHING CAN SAVE YOU NOW!
SUPERMAN FAMILY ADVENTURES
BALTAZAR FRANCO
SUPER-PETS!
WHY ARE YOU FOLLOWING ME?!
only from...
STONE ARCH BOOKS™
a capstone imprint www.capstonepub.com

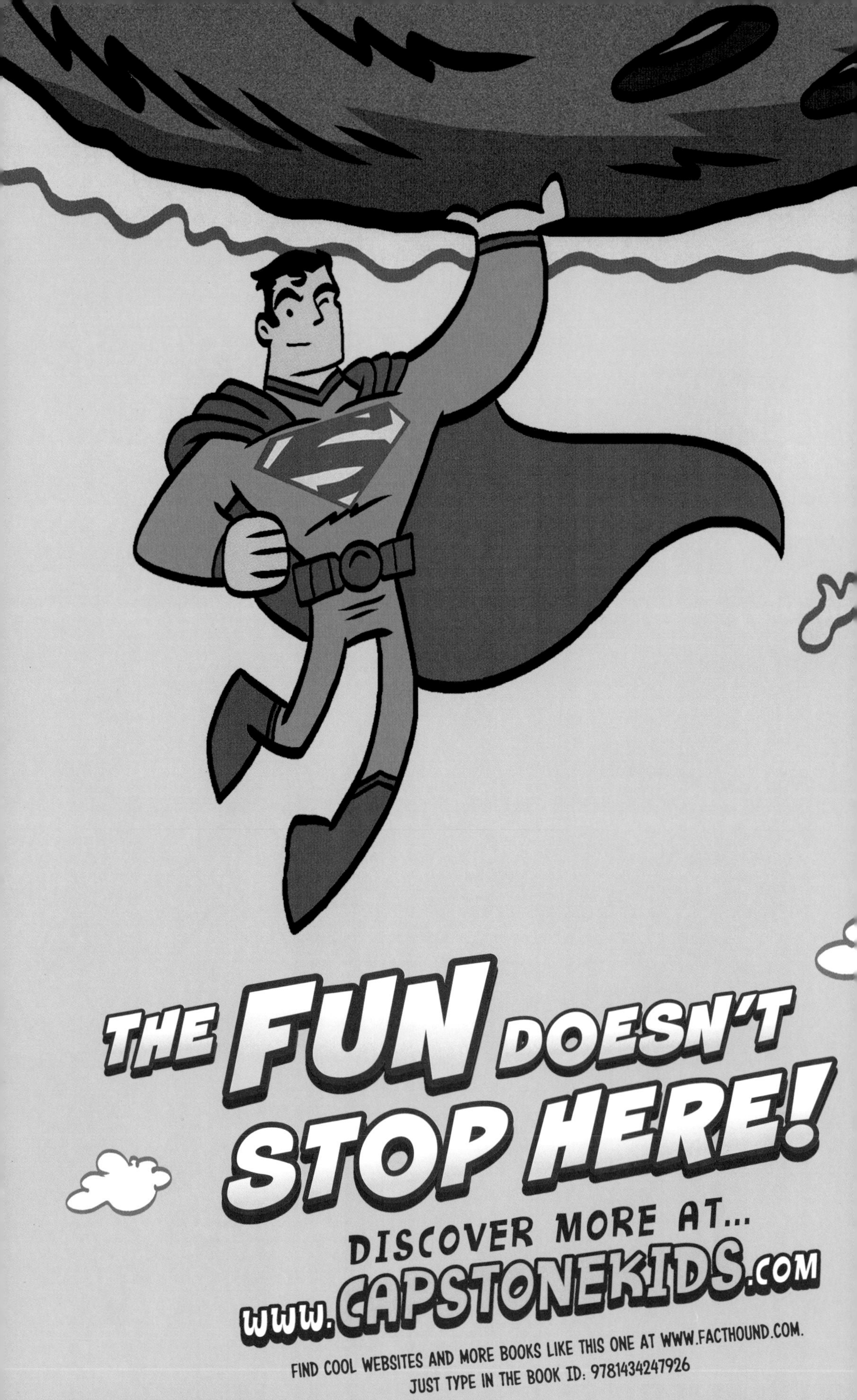